FROM THE LIFE

To Al

From the Life

and other stories

Siân Preece

Polygon

Polygon
An imprint of Edinburgh University Press Ltd
22 George Square, Edinburgh

Typeset in Galliard by
Hewer Text Ltd, Edinburgh, and
printed and bound in Great Britain by
Bell & Bain Ltd, Glasgow

A CIP Record for this book is
available from the British Library

ISBN 0 7486 6264 2 (paperback)

The Publisher acknowledges subsidy from

towards the publication of this volume.

Contents

Acknowledgements

MANY, MANY THANKS to Alan Spence, without whom this book would not have been written. Respect due! Thanks also to Marion Sinclair, and to Alison Bowden and Jeanie Scott at Polygon for all their help and advice. I am grateful to the Scottish Arts Council for their generous and timely bursary.

Agoraphobix

THE DOOR TO THE launderette banged open. A teenage boy bundled in with an empty basket and shook the rain from his black hair.

'Bonjour, m'mselle!'

'Bonjour, m'sieur.'

A first-ever moustache blurred his upper lip. I ducked my head and rattled the pages of my book, but he didn't want a conversation.

I'd already had a visit from Old Resistance Lady. Today she had re-created a fight or a country dance, leaping and gesticulating, her hat askew and her stockings concertina'd around her birds' ankles. The story had ended with a feast, or some enjoyable dentistry. Her son caused her to weep and sigh, and many of her friends had died by firing squad, or fishing. I nodded noncommittally: 'Ah oui?'

With her finger to her lips, she reminded me, as ever, that she had been in the Resistance, and her eyes cast about for collaborators behind the dryers. She hissed 'Au revoir!' as if it was a code that only we knew.

The boy unloaded clumsy armfuls of damp laundry into his basket. A thick mist boiled from the washing machine, steam and cooking oil. I recognised him from the Moroccan restaurant next door. His washing was all napkins, dishcloths and rags, transparent with grease; none of the sweet smell of fresh laundry.

'Wash them again!' I thought, but he hoisted the basket to one of the dryers and tipped them in haphazardly, not really looking. I wondered what he was thinking of instead. He slammed the dryer door, slammed it again to be sure, then pressed a handful of coins into the slot.

'Au'voir.' A nod.

'M'sieur.'

Alone again.

My own washing still had a while to go. I hated doing the laundry. I hated our one-room apartment. I hated France. We'd had a fight about it that morning, and now I hated Ed as well. He was a

selfish bastard

and it was

all right for him: he got out to work; he *talked* to people! I was stuck in this rats' paradise every day

but that was just

my mother talking, could I hear myself? Mew mew mew

yeah, but

my mother hadn't followed her man's career around the world like Tammy-sodding-Wynette, and furthermore

did I think it was fun for him? He couldn't order a fucking sandwich here, never mind push his research forward

and furthermore

no-one says 'furthermore'

if he could manage not to interrupt for a

interrupt!

for a second, he hadn't spent the last two days bug-spraying the apartment! The stuff was probably carcinogenic

not like my twenty-a-day habit, oh no

but

no wonder I smoked! It was on my CV under 'Leisure Activities'; smoking, drinking, and trotting after my husband like a lost gosling

so

what did I want to do? What did I *want*?

I didn't know.

* * *

Alone in the apartment, my own anger wheeled and turned on me, leaving me shaking. I submerged it in a fit of cleaning, hating myself for being like my mother; polishing her frustration into the shine of the dining-room table, justifying herself with her impeccable housekeeping. I cleaned until even the radio noise seemed untidy, and all that remained was the laundry bag, fat and full. I would have to take it down and wash it.

I would have to Go Out.

Going Out was not a casual undertaking. I wondered if I was becoming agoraphobic. I had an idea that there was a character in *Asterix* called Agoraphobix. Not in French, though; the names were different, like Tin Tin's dog being Milou instead of Snowy. I would have to go to the library in the Carré Curiale and look it up. Hope no-one spoke to me.

To face the journey to the launderette I tooled up with my 'security'. Outsized dark glasses, my cheap knock-off Walkman from Carrefour, a book, fags and matches. There was only one shop in Chambéry that sold British cigarettes; the shopkeeper called me 'Seelk Cut'. I put on my don't-talk-to-me coat, its turned-up collar reassuringly high, and a baseball cap. Last week, a teenage girl had shouted 'Michael Jackson!' in the street and it was possible that she had meant me.

On the way, I stopped to check my reflection in a parked car. The car was too big for the narrow medieval street; a dark dragon, come to terrify the Savoisiens with its mirrored eyes. The rain had covered it with wet beads, shining and rainbowed, a swarm of tiny black beetles over its gleaming sides. I ran my finger through them, and the droplets scattered and regrouped, making a ragged line that pleased me against all that perfection. It enhanced it somehow, like a tendril of hair curled on a bare shoulder.

I drew a swirl around the door handle, marvelling at the streamlining, and peered in the driver's window to see, not my own face, but the car's owner looking back at me.

'Alors?'

A young black man, with dark glasses like my own; our noses almost touched.

'Pardon!'

I dropped my washing, picked it up again, and shrugged in apology. He laughed, reassured that I was harmless, and gunned the engine to impress me.

I hid in the launderette and watched until he drove away. My embarrassment made me feel hot and sick; but the shrug! I was proud of that shrug. It had felt very natural and French. I was becoming bilingual in body language at least.

Now I rubbed a hole in the launderette's steamy window. The rain had laid off a bit so I went out for a smoke. Smoking was company. Standing in the street looked sad, but standing in the street to smoke had purpose. It was a bad habit like drinking, but you could do it all day. In Chambéry, people smoked everywhere. In the summer, girls lay topless and lit up by the lake, but my eyes watered at the thought of it; the dropped ash, the give-away matchbooks that spat cinders when you struck them. In the winter they smoked in the supermarkets and food shops. The British tourists, in Savoie for the skiing, would tut and flap, and stamp off to look for 'proper sliced bread' and food wrapped in plastic. We called them 'Eurotrash', but it broke our homesick hearts to hear them speak English.

I whispered the Welsh word for it, '*hiraeth*', and the smoke curled and turned on me. Hiraeth. Homesick and then some. Like the song, 'We'll kiss away each hour of hiraeth when you come home again to Wales.' But Wales wasn't home any more, either. My cigarette burned down. I stood, alone and dispossessed, and it started to rain again.

Back in the launderette I settled down on the clothes-folding table and checked my watch. Ed should be stepping off the bus soon. Five minutes' walk from the terminus, past the Four Elephants fountain, and he would come this way. I'd wave and smile, setting the tone for a reconciliation, for us to talk. We could carry the washing home together. The launderette radio played a song by Les Ritas Mitsouko. I recognised it from the album we had at home and sang along, pleased that I knew the words.

'On n'a pas que de l'amour; ça non . . . 'y a d'la haîne!' A nice, peppy tune about hate. Catherine Ringer's scratch of a voice reprimanded me:

'Soyons plus positifs.'

Positive!

I opened my book and arranged the rest of my stuff around me on the table, my coat and bag forming a nest, a small space for me. I sat in it with my feet up, feeling cosy and self-contained and not unhappy. I'd been down for so long that it surprised me. But I was okay. No-one was bothering me. It wasn't an active feeling, I had yet to nurture myself to that state, but it was a start. Ed was right. It was up to me to choose what I wanted.

It was warm in the launderette, and bright, but the oily smell was getting thicker. I hopped up to take a look at the dryer. The boy's napkins flipflopped to their own dual rhythm in the dark, pitted drum. At their centre was a light effect like sparks, twinkling and starry. They were just starting to smoulder.

'Shit!'

I put my hand to the dryer door, stopped myself. I thought of simply leaving the launderette, escaping, but my own washing was still trapped in the rinse cycle. I ran out to the Moroccan restaurant, faltered halfway when I remembered my purse still on the table, ran on anyway and banged at the back door. The boy was sitting at the kitchen table, carefully cutting pictures out of a skiing magazine, his chin lowered, frowning. He looked up and I shouted,

'La launderette!' La? Le? No, '-ette', feminine ending, la. I shouted again, 'Les serviettes! Vite!'

He looked confused, then his eyes flicked wide and he leapt up and rushed out past me, the photos whirling in his wake, cut-out arms of paper waving after him.

We skidded into the launderette in a cartoon-panic. The boy dragged the dryer door open and the napkins burst into flames, fed by the inrush of air. He snatched them out, wailing, and we stamped on them frenziedly, wordlessly, dancing in the acrid smoke. They re-ignited like trick birthday candles until we thought of kicking them out into the wet street, where they hissed and floated in the gutter. A woman passing by said 'Ohh, là là là!' and dragged away her dog, who wanted to investigate. The boy stared at the napkins, horrified, turned his back on them and looked to the sky. He didn't want to see them. He turned again, threw his hands in the air, 'No-on!'; a man's anger with a boy's dark, frightened eyes. I helped him pick through the napkins, looking for an undamaged one that I could offer to comfort him, lacking the words. An older man came rolling out of the restaurant and began shouting at him and, as he did, Ed rounded the corner.

'What the hell's this?'

'There was a fire; we put it out.' I wiped my face with my arm and smelt smoke. Ed wiped a smut from my face. I said, 'I figured out what I want to do. I want to be a firewoman!' I was laughing as I said it, and Ed laughed too.

'Heck, why not!'

The sun had come out, sharpening the smell of the street; grass and wet dust, and pine blown down from the mountains. Groups of children emerged from the school like flowers opening, dressed in bright colours. They shouldered Disney rucksacks stuffed with graph-paper *cahiers*, and chattered with their special brand of authority and earnestness. Ed carried the washing over one shoulder, and held my hand as we walked. Old Resistance Lady came out to sweep the rainwater from her balcony, and a cat on the floor below jumped up at the shower she created and licked his shoulder, outraged.

Back home, we hung the washing on the shower-curtain rail to dry. We ate a makeshift dinner of canned cassoulet, sticky and rich, and finished off a plastic litre bottle of red wine. I speculated on what the boy was doing now . . .

. . . his father was telling the story to the customers. It was a big joke; or it was a wicked waste. As the boy passed by in his waiter's jacket, his father reached out and ruffled his hair; or he reached out and cuffed him. Later, in their small, noisy apartment with the green metal shutters, the boy would lie on his bed and plan to run away; or he would dream of girls and skiing, and look in the mirror for his moustache.

It was dark now. I looked for my reflection in the balcony window, but there was only steam from the drying clothes. We drew pictures in it. I drew a stickman jumping on some burning napkins. Ed gave him a speech bubble, 'Oh là-là!' We started a window conversation, set ourselves the rule of only using three words.

That poor boy!

These things always. Happen to you.

That was cheating.

I don't care.

I paused and looked at him.

How are you?

I am okay. How are you?

I am okay.

Another pause. He took a slug of wine, wrote,

Fed up here.

Oui, moi aussi.

Let's go Brit.

Go Brit where?

Don't know. Scotland?

Scotland is cool.

Scotland is cold!

Damn cold here!

Yeah, damn right.

I ran out of space and moved to the next window.

You for real?

If you are.

Do it, then?

Do it, then.

The weight of the words became too much; they broke the

surface tension, dribbled and ran. In the morning, cold and hungover, I breathed on the glass and the words came back again, 'Scotland?', and a stickman jumping on a fire of napkins and, through the window, snow.

Running Out

MY MOTHER ONCE told me of a village that drowned.

'The people were all right,' she said quickly; I was small then, and it was important to me that people be all right. 'They moved away.'

'Where did they go?'

'Scattered far and wide.'

She looked towards the window as if they would be out there, walking down the street with their suitcases. It sounded like a story, but she said it was true.

'Did the people want to go?'

'No, they didn't want to go.'

'Why did they, then?'

'They had to. The valley was needed for a reservoir. A big lake,' she explained, 'To keep water in, for people to use.'

'The people in the village?'

'No, English people,' and she frowned.

'But what happened to the houses?'

'The houses are still there, under the water.'

I tried to imagine it; a house like my nan's, with the china dogs still fierce on the mantlepiece, and seaweed curtains waving in the green water. Tea cosies like jelly fish, rugs like rays swimming over coral-bed sofas. There would be no point in closing the doors; you could just float out of the window and look down on the map of your garden, at the whole village under water like a present from the seaside. Tryweryn. Cwm Atlantis.

A tap turns in Liverpool, and a church steeple breaks the surface of a Welsh lake.

I hear a chime like a church bell under water . . . it's the chain of the bath plug, dancing under the hot tumble at my feet. I turn off the tap and lean back, relax. At the other end of the bath, my toes bob up, white in the red water; ten little croutons in a bowl of tomato soup. I feel hot and weak. I feel as if I will be in this water forever.

At first I felt like a pervert, walking the streets of Cardiff at dusk with a Welsh costume concealed under my mac. Red skirt, checked shawl and apron. A scaled-up version of my St David's Day outfit at school; but no pungent, dusty daffodil pinned to my chest, just a flattened yellow fake. I kept my tall black hat in a carrier bag, swinging it like a bucket, until I got to work. Our boss had no shame, making us dress like that.

In the alley behind the restaurant, I told Jackie: 'The Welsh costume's all made up anyway.'

'Oh aye?' She picked a wad of chewing gum from her mouth and held it in her fingers while she dragged on her fag. Her face was pointed and modern over the white pussycat bow at her chin.

'Aye, it was all invented by this English woman. We used to wear little round bonnets like everyone else. I remember it from History.'

'Well, don't tell Alwyn.' Alwyn was the restaurant owner. 'He've only just found one to fit your big head.'

'Well, that's 'cause I've got big brains. Your hat must be titchy.' I pretended to read a label at the back. 'Look! "Age five!"'

'Ha bloody ha.'

In the kitchen window, froggy, pink fingers appeared and rubbed a squeaky hole in the steam. It was Fat Benny, the bald, wordless washer-up, spying on us. Fat Benny was in love with girls.

'Hiya, darlin'!' Jackie tinkled piano fingers at him. 'Meet you behind the bins after for a snog!'

Fat Benny's eye winked shyly in the peephole he had made. He pressed soft, round kisses on the window; wrinkled Os.

'Aw, Jackie, don't tease him.'

'Why not? He's a creepy git.'

I shushed her with my hands. 'He's not creepy. He's just sad.'

Fat Benny bobbed around in the kitchen window, looking quite happy to be sad.

Alwyn pounced out of the kitchen door.

'Have you laid them tables yet? Come on girls, chop chop.'

We had laid the tables when we got in, but Alwyn hated to see us doing nothing. In the kitchen he tried to arrange the two of us into a line, then stood before us with his tiny feet, in their tasselled shoes, at a perfect ten-to-two.

'Jackie, you're meeting and greeting and taking orders. Rhian, you're taking coats and showing to tables. And Rhian,' he added, 'better not do any serving, is it? Not with the way you dish out soup.'

He was being bitchy and I stared at him under the brim of my hat, giving him attitude, but he turned away.

It was getting that Alwyn took another job off me every night. He was right about the soup, though. If I was carrying it, there was no point putting it in a bowl; it always ended up in the serving plate, with the doily drinking it like a Kleenex. And I couldn't manage vegetables that were too round; the peas would make a break for it, and I could only keep the potatoes on the plate if they were mashed. I spent most of my time in the kitchen, scraping butter from a big plastic vat into individual china pots. The trick to getting the butter smooth on top was to breathe on it, to warm it, but I didn't let Alwyn see that.

At the end of the night, Chef would give us left-overs to take home. Fat Benny would only take bread.

'Go on, Fat Benny, there's a lonely Glamorgan sausage here without a butty. Or how about this salmon steak? Lovely bit of fish; the skin's come off is all.'

But Fat Benny would shake his head and look as if he were going to cry.

'All right. Bread it is.'

And we would tumble the brown, floury rolls into Fat Benny's Adidas bag.

'He do look all right on it, though,' said Jackie.

'He looks like an autopsy,' said Chef; and these two things meant that Jackie didn't like Benny, and Chef did.

There's a bottle of vodka on the edge of the bath, incongruous beside the two shampoos. Mine is Plus-Conditioner-for-Damaged-Hair, with a picture of, I think, a vitamin on the side. Dad's is Anti-Dandruff, with a static dribble of turquoise paste obscuring the letters. His razors are rusty and leaking, sitting in a pool of their own orange blood.

Tonight I showed Fat Benny how to make napkins into shapes.

'Want to see a crown?'

He nodded, wedged in the corner, keeping his bum warm on the oven. I flapped the napkin open, folded and pinched, folded again.

Jackie was serving in the restaurant and Alwyn was going round the tables, talking to the customers. He did it to emphasise that he was the owner, a businessman, *crachach*, not an employee like his little waitresses. When he said, 'We hope you enjoy your meal,' the 'we' was practically royal.

Alwyn divided the customers into two categories: the first was the Smart Regulars, who were rich, and used to eating out, and didn't bother to dress up for it. Alwyn would rub his hands and smile at them like he had greased his teeth.

His second category was the Special Occasions. These were the people who had saved up, and came dressed in their best, most uncomfortable clothes for the treat. The men had big hands with scrubbed, raw knuckles. The women wore perfume that made me sneeze. They cringed silently in their seats, spooked by the sound of their plain conversation in this chichi, unfamiliar place. When Alwyn talked to them, they stared at him like cats, and whispered when he'd gone: 'That was the owner.' He always sat the Special Occasions by the toilets.

Jackie's categories were Good Tippers and Bad Tippers.

My categories were Human and Inhuman, depending on how they treated us.

I was supposed to be microwaving the Welsh cakes so they'd feel fresh-from-the-oven warm. Chef had disabled the timer to stop it going 'ping' and giving the game away, so you had to watch it.

'There you go.'

I gave Fat Benny the napkin crown and he perched it on his shiny head, did a little dance. His big, melon face split into a ripe smile and he made his laugh sound, a high-pitched, soprano wheeze.

'Now we've both got hats,' I said, and we grinned at each other.

Chef had finished up and gone home by this time. I had nothing to do except wait until Alwyn called for the Welsh cakes. I checked the bow on my hat so I'd be ready straight away; Alwyn was always saying, 'It's not the customers' job to wait; it's our job to wait on them.'

I used to complain to Jackie that, if I found the Restaurant Management book where he read that, I'd burn it. But tonight, when I looked around the kitchen at the white tiles streaked with rainbows of detergent, and the family of knives hanging from Grandpa to Baby on the wall, I thought: I wouldn't mind doing this. Creating this order, this cleanliness. I could go back to college and do Hotel and Restaurant Management. Food Hygiene. Catering.

'What do you think, Benny? Could I do Restaurant Management?'

Benny widened his eyes. He breathed in as if about to cough and, in a high, girl's whisper, said:

'The bread's not for me, it's for my mam. She do soak it in milk. It's her teeth, see.'

He put his hand to his mouth, astonished at himself, and we stared at each other. I had never heard him speak before, and now

I realised with surprise that he was quite young: perhaps nineteen or twenty. I didn't know what to do. Did he want me to congratulate him, or would it just make him shy? It felt like giving someone a card when you're not sure it's their birthday.

'Benny,' I said, unfolding another napkin, 'Do you want to see a swan?'

Benny's mam.

She has Benny's ham arms, encased in the sleeves of a floral dress, and the same bald head in a curly wig. She is as silent as her son; they communicate telepathically, watch sit-coms with the sound down, and laugh so only dogs can hear.

When my own mother left, I used to imagine her going back to her drowned village. Walking into the water in her dress, the skirts billowing around her as she dived and searched for her house; or crying on the shore like a mermaid, her hair streaming. But my dad said she'd found a new boyfriend in Merthyr.

Alwyn came into the kitchen, rubbing his hands together briskly like a fly.

'Where have all the napkins gone?' he said, then, 'Ah, Rhian, have you done with them Welsh cakes?'

I pressed the catch and the microwave door sprang open as if the Welsh cakes had rebelled and were kicking their way out. But they were safe, tanned and toasty under the hygienic kitchen neon. They slid wilfully on the plate, but I corralled them against my chest, sprinkled them and my daffodil with a shower of sugar, and offered them for Alwyn's inspection.

'Well, they look fine,' he said. He chose one, snapped it open, and we watched as a currant gave up its last puff of moisture. The cakes were burnt, dry, as solid as shortcake.

'Oh no! Oh Alwyn, I'm sorry!'

Alwyn took the plate from me. He tipped the cakes and their greasy, sugared doily into the pedal bin, and we heard them scuttling like coal to the bottom. Without looking at Benny, Alwyn handed him the plate for washing and, when he finally spoke, flecks of spittle sparked from his mouth.

'Look, Rhian . . .'

'I'll do some more! It won't take a minute.'

'No, no, don't bother. Just . . . take the dessert trolley out, will you?'

There was only one table left now, or rather two, pushed together for a party: businessmen from London, in Cardiff for a conference. We got more English customers here than Welsh. They came for the love spoons decorating the wall, the spinning wheel in the corner, for Jackie and me sweating in our tall hats. There must have been photographs of us all over the country: two life-size peg dollies with eyes scalded red by the camera flash.

'Say cheese!'

'No, say "caws"! That's Welsh for "cheese!"' Alwyn was taking an evening class at the university.

I had taken the businessmen's coats to the cloakroom and, alone in the dark, stroked the collars and cuffs, slotted my hands into the flat, empty pockets. Next to those tiny stitches, my own clothes felt as clumsy as a doll's.

Jackie had smelt money, and now I heard her laughing with the men, responding to their banter; giggling for tips where I would have tried for a smart answer. I wobbled the trolley towards them, the thick carpet catching in its wheels, jingling the dishes and making the trifle tremble as if it were afraid. The noise seemed vulgar. I was ashamed.

'Here's Blodwen Mark Two!', shouted a man at the head of the table.

'Hello, Blodwen!'

Jackie muttered to me through her clenched smile, 'We've got a right lot here; they're calling me Blodwen too;' then 'You've got cream all up your shawl.'

The shawls got into everything. I wiped the cream off with my apron and parked the trolley.

'Good evening! Tonight we have sherry trifle, lemon meringue pie, apple tart and custard . . .'

One of the men pulled me by the strings of my apron to stand next to him.

'Never mind the meringues, Blodwen; give us a song!' He

smelt of brandy and cigars, and rich-food farts. There was a splash of dried gravy on his chin.

'I can't sing!' I smiled to soften the refusal.

'Nonsense; all you Welsh can sing. Come on!' He started banging the table, waved at the others to join in:

'Song! Song! Song!'

I glanced around the table in a panic; the faces of the men ran together, became a film, a flicker picture of one man ageing. In his twenties, the shoulders still firm, the hint of a squash racquet in the back of the company car. Then the weight of seniority silting down through the years, the tailoring becoming more careful to hide the bulk. A daring, last-chance moustache at fifty, the word 'distinguished' starting to apply, then the silver hair, the golden handshake, and first-name terms with the doctor. The same man, the same men; a row of grey cloth with a shared mission statement – only the coloured ties, like a Warhol print, to tell them apart.

One of the men spoke, and the picture refracted again.

'Steady on!' he said slowly, his words chewy with alcohol. 'The girlie's trying to do her job.'

The first man replied as if I wasn't there: 'Don't worry. I'll leave her an enormous tip.'

I heard myself shout, in a furious rush,

'All right! I'll give you a song!'

They cheered, with no idea that I was angry, or even that I could be. I folded my hands across my apron like a trembling bird, and began to sing:

'There was an old farmer who sat on a rock,

A-waving and shaking his big hairy . . .'

I was into the second verse when Alwyn came screaming out of the kitchen like a fire engine in tasselled shoes and dragged me away.

'What do you think you're doing!' A purple vein twitched on his red temple.

'They asked for a song.'

'Good God!' He threw his arms in the air and I flinched, although he'd had no intention of hitting me. Benny cowered in the corner, frantically washing and re-washing a clean plate, as Alwyn marched up and down the kitchen, his little feet pit-patting on the tiles, repeating his mantra: 'The good restaurateur remains calm at all times.' Then he turned to me and took a deep breath.

'Listen,' he said, 'this job, well, it hasn't really been working out, has it?'

I felt sick and serious. My hands filled with sweat, dripping cold between my hot fingers.

'I'm sorry!' I said. 'I'll do better in future, honest I will!'

He shook his head. 'I'm sorry,' he said, echoing me, 'I've already spoken to another girl who worked here before. See, her husband's left her and she needs the money. We're having her back.' He looked at me and added slowly, to be sure that I understood, 'Instead of you.' The way he said it, I knew he'd practised it. I knew it was a lie.

'*I* need the money,' I said, but Alwyn had already turned his eyes down, dismissing me.

'You're young,' he said. 'You'll find another job, easy. I'll put a bit extra in your last wage packet. Okay? All right? All right, then. Off you go now, and bring the uniform back any time you like. By Thursday, at least. And have it cleaned, will you? There's cream all up the shawl.'

I saw Benny's face like a snapshot, mournful and melting in the background. My bag was hanging on the back of the door, hidden in a row of coats on their hooks, and I pulled at it, tugged in sudden fury until the whole lot came down with a sound like snow falling from a roof. I saw my own mac sprawled under the pile of headless bodies and hauled it out. Its empty arms embraced me as I ran.

I saw a postcard once: a woman lying in a river with all her clothes on, and flowers. Now I unpin my fake daffodil, the pin resisting in the wet tweed, and hold it to my chest. The shawl is heavy with water, I feel its weight when I move my shoulders. It has become crimson where it was white before.

The water has cooled again. I let it out and run more hot, and swill my skirt around to see the dye billowing scarlet. The best, though, is the hat; the steam has broken it down, the brim is collapsing on to my face. Little flecks of black felt are breaking off and floating in the water, like the specks you see in your eye when you're tired; or like water-boatmen, who dent the smooth, wet light with their insect feet. They scatter in the breath of my laughter. Even a smile seems to move them.

I stand up in the bath and the water pours from me in a loud wave, then slows to a trickle. The clothes are heavy, but supporting their weight makes me feel strong, defiant.

I pull the plug, and the red water starts running out.

Thass not a Problem

'I LERRED ENGLISH,' said the Taiwanese girl. 'Shourra lerred French.'

She bounced on the futon, a brightly-coloured circus girl riding on an elephant; but her gypsy hands were business-like, feeling for lumps, and I knew she would try to talk me down.

'Issa pretty colour, pink!' she said, so firmly that she could have meant not just the futon, but pink in general. 'Let's stretch it out, huh?'

'I've got a bad back,' I said, thinking of the red-wine stains that were folded like shadows into the mattress, but she flung up her hands and snatched around her head at invisible birds.

'Thass not a problem! You help me out!'

'Okay!'

We laid the futon flat and she made me lie beside her to check the size. I smelt the cumin and lime of her sweat as she reached above her head.

'Oh yeah, room for two!' she said. 'I'm gonna get a boyfriend, real soon!' Something else on her list of Things to Buy in Montreal. She drummed her feet, two canary-coloured sandals fluttering up and down on the mattress, and her Mickey Mouse rucksack, bulging with textbooks, slid to the floor with a nylon sigh.

'What are you studying?'

'Business.' Buz–i–ness. 'I'm in the University, the pretty good one.'

'My husband teaches there!' I wished he could come home now and see me lying on the futon with the Taiwanese girl. She turned her head and spoke loudly in my ear, making the fine hairs hum.

'You going back to England?'

'Scotland. Yeah.'

'Too much fuckin' politics in Quebec, huh?'

'No, just . . . homesick.'

'Yeah, I'm sick of it too!' She jumped up, smoothed her dolly clothes, and I struggled up beside her like a horse, kicking for leverage.

'So,' she said, 'thirty bucks!'

'We're actually asking forty . . .'

'No, thirty; look, you got blood on it!'

'That's red wine – oops! Okay, thirty-five.'

'Thirty-three. Iss lucky, two numbers the same!'

I turned my palms towards her, 'Yeah, okay,' and my futon suddenly belonged to someone else. 'How will you get it back?' She would ride it down the street in a parade, twirling a baton.

'Thass not a problem! I come back tonight with my friend, pay you then. Don't you sell it to no-one else!'

'No way!'

I took her down to the front door and watched her pirouette along the kerb to the bus stop. She stood waving at me like an old friend until I turned away.

Through the office window, Mrs Sirussi and Bob were arguing from the waist up, like Punch and Judy. Bob was charcoal-sketched, a Picasso bull, black grime in the lines of his face. Mrs Sirussi's wig ruffled indignantly and her spectacles, on a chain around her neck, peered wildly down her hen's bosom.

'You fix up those drains before we're in water to our asses!' She swiped at Bob with a rolled-up envelope, and he ducked aside.

'Drains! You don't know *jack* about drains!' As the janitor, he got his apartment for free, but he had no natural feeling for cleanliness, for what needed to be done. He slept most of the day and spent his evenings in the bar across the street. 'I'll tell ya about *drains*!' he added, but that seemed to be his final word; he spotted me through the window and cantered out, falling into step beside me. Mrs Sirussi made obscene shadow-puppet gestures at him through the bug screen.

'China girl!' said Bob. 'Very nice.'

'She's buying our stuff,' I said, startled that he'd been watching us.

'Hey! Maybe *I* want to buy your stuff too!'

Please, no. 'Sure!' He was my height, but stocky; a cartoon fat man with truncated fingers that seemed too numerous for his hands. In the lobby, he pulled down our advert, looking for a moment as if he would eat it, and stubbed a finger at the stick picture of our furniture.

'Maybe I wanna buy that table'n'*chairs*!' he said angrily. 'Maybe I should *see* that table'n'chairs! What colour is it?'

'White.'

'We'll fix that,' he said.

On the way up the stairs, I planned how to disable him. The kitchen knives were packed away; I would smash the phone into his face, break a chair across his back, a movie stunt, and tip his body down the stairwell.

'Maybe you could *split* those chairs!' he said, making me jump; but then he added: 'I just need two for me and my boy.'

'I didn't know you had a boy.'

'Hey! I gotta boy! Maybe he'll come'n'*stay* with me sometime! He c'n sit on the other *chair*.'

He pulled a photograph out of his pocket; a spindly kid frowned nervously at the camera, an outsized 'Canadiens' hockey shirt hanging on his shrugged shoulders. The picture was creased and fixed with Scotch tape, faded with filth like an Old Master.

'My boy!' said Bob, as amazed as I was that this skinny child was his. 'He's nine now. Phew! Did ya have to live at the *top*?'

I waited at the open door while Bob, on all fours, nosed and snorted under the table, inspecting it. He looked so like a bull that I was surprised when he stood on his hind legs and wiped his forehead with a rough, scrubbing motion. Thinking.

'Thirty bucks?'

'Twenty-five,' I said, getting the haggling wrong, but he shook his slow, steer's head.

'Thirty. I'll give ya five now and the rest on *Friday*. I'll be *straight* by Friday. I'll take it then.'

Our flight was on Saturday; the timing was perfect.

'Okay.'

He shook my hand and I thought of judo throws, but his grip was gentle, and I saw that his grimace was a smile. When he'd gone I flapped a dishcloth and sprayed perfume, but his earthy smell still haunted the room. I opened all the windows and went out for a walk.

The pavement was warm, pumiced pale grey by the sun. Six months ago I had come out into the first flock of snow and watched the people learning how to walk in it again, their arms windmilling in heavy coat sleeves. Outside the 7-Eleven I had found the shape of a flurried, fallen snow angel and followed its trail, splash by scarlet splash, to the steps of the Queen Elizabeth Hospital. The blood refused to clot in the cold, and passers-by kicked it into atoms in the snow.

Now it was as hot as a different country. The smell of coffee and car fumes hung in the still air and, outside the pavement cafés, all the couples were in love. The cat who thought he owned the second-hand bookshop sat in the doorway, blinking graciously as customers stepped over him. We had sold our books here in a job lot. I went in and picked a familiar spine off the shelf, remembered the creak when the pages had been new, the smell of fresh ink and glue. On the way out I kissed my finger and rubbed it on the cat's head to say 'goodbye', but he just yawned and shook the mark of my caress from his fur, scattering mites of dust in the sunlight.

It was so hot that Mrs Sirussi had taken her wig off. She stood waiting for me with her hair in pin curls, pressed into damp shapes on her skull. Her jailer's keys hung at her waist, and she performed a small arrest on my elbow:

'Come! Come see!'

I knew she wanted to show me Bob's apartment in the basement. She often tried to show me the other apartments in the block while the occupants were out, and sometimes there was a hint of scent in our rooms, a disturbance of dust that meant she had been there, too.

'Come!' she insisted, 'See what I have to put up with!'

There were things wrong with his door: kick-scuffs at the base, drunken scratches around the lock. Mrs Sirussi opened it with her mop of keys and shouldered it, the wood shuddering as she pushed against the rubbish inside. The air rushed out like damp cave-breath, and we stepped into the room.

'My God!' I whispered, 'It's full of bats!'

Bob's four walls shimmered and twitched with a thousand wings, shining, layered like wet tiles on a roof; but the room was dark, the blinds nailed shut, and Mrs Sirussi said:

'What's with the bats? Those're photographs! Look.'

It was the boy I had seen in Bob's picture, over and over; cramming his toddler mouth with Teddy Grahams, clutching a hockey stick taller than he was, sitting on the lap of a woman whose head had been carefully cut away. A lot of the photographs had been copied, arranged so that no two copies would be together. They were so closely packed, you couldn't have put a finger between them.

'What sort of maniac does that!' clucked Mrs Sirussi. She picked her way through a cityscape of pizza boxes and beer cans, her hands pecking about in a displaced cleaning gesture. I couldn't see where Bob was going to fit a table'n'chairs in here, let alone a boy.

'Lookit this! Look!' Mrs Sirussi pushed the bathroom door, and I saw that the bath was full of cold, grey water, scummed with a lichen of soap and skin. A drip plocked from the tap, disturbing the Celtic knotwork of curled hairs on the surface. 'He needs his ass kicking, that's what he needs!'

My eyes were getting used to the gloom now; on one of the photos I saw lip prints over the boy's face, kisses that had dried to a smudge.

'He must love his kid,' I said.

'Love his kid! Oh, yeah! He hasn't seen that kid in five years. He hit him upside the head with a bottle, and the wife got a restraining order.'

'No!' Bob's square, dirty hand shaking mine, enclosing it . . . 'Has he ever, you know . . . shown any violence towards you?'

'Whaat? He better not! That's all I say!' She squinted at the blinds, snorted, the way Bob had at the table; then suddenly, furiously, she grabbed at the corner of a blind and tore it down. The room, which had just been a mess until then, became dangerous and frightening in the exposing light. I was sickened by how Bob lived, had to get out. I left Mrs Sirussi throwing boxes about, sweeping beer cans to the ground with her arm, making a carnival of noise.

The evening came, and Bob still hadn't returned. I left the door open to hear when he came in, and packed books into boxes while Chris filled the picture holes in the wall with toothpaste. The walls were pale blue, and we'd had to buy *Crest* to match the colour.

'I don't *care*,' said Chris. 'She should never have been in his apartment. She's not our house-mother, she's our landlady. People have a right to their privacy. It's part of the deal.'

'What if it's a health hazard, though?'

'Then she should call the *Régie*.' Voice of Reason.

'It is, though. A health hazard, I mean. And Mrs S went *ape*, just tore his blinds down and started kicking stuff around. I don't know why she doesn't throw him out.'

'Well, you can't in Canada,' said Chris. 'There's a law: you can't throw a tenant out unless you have a relative who needs the room. I remember, one of my students had a fight with her landlord; the next thing, he's got this alleged daughter coming from Ontario, and the student gets a month's notice.'

'What a scam! But we should tell Mrs S, maybe she could do that with Bob.'

Chris squeezed a pea of toothpaste on to his finger, rubbed it into the wall.

'Perhaps they have a love–hate relationship!' he said.

'Brr – creepy!'

'Well, he's buying our table, and then we'll never see him again.' He sniffed his fingers. 'Minty-fresh!'

It was still hot at nine when the Taiwanese girl came back, leading her friend by the hand.

'You must be the husband!' she told Chris. 'I must be Wei Wei! And this is Shabmyn – she's my muscle!'

Shabmyn nodded, her eyes solemn behind her thick spectacles. She had a large head on a frail body, like a baby bird, with a beaky overbite. Chris looked at the futon, then at the two tiny girls, and I saw him squaring his shoulders, becoming the Big Man.

'Don't worry!' He patted my back. 'We'll do it!'

'Oh, *thanks*!' I said, but Wei Wei shook her head.

'We are two strong women!' she said, and they hoisted the futon up, getting it as far as the top step before its weight overwhelmed them. It tipped over, and the momentum carried them squealing and yelling downstairs to the first landing. There was a crash, then silence. We leaned over the banister anxiously, but there was no sign of the girls, just the futon, wedged at an angle. They had hit the light on the way down, and it swayed horribly in the sea-sick stairwell.

'Ahoy!' I shouted, and a muffled voice called back from under the futon.

'Hello! Iss okay! Iss good like this, very quick! Maximises our productivity!'

'She's studying business,' I told Chris. The futon seemed to shuffle on of its own accord, then took a second plunge down the stairs.

'You got the money, didn't you?' said Chris.

'Thass not a problem!' I said.

'Eh?'

'Here – thirty-three bucks.'

'We said forty . . .'

Through the window we watched them set upon the waiting cab driver, mobbing him until he agreed to push the futon into the back seat; driving off with the door open and Shabmyn perched on the mattress, digging her claws in. They were gone, the futon was gone, the apartment was strange and echoing. Four years in Montreal: a jigsaw, completed, the last piece pushed in to make a picture. Now we were taking it apart again, scattering the pieces around the city. Someone would read our books, would wake in the morning and turn on our bedside lamp. Someone would move into this apartment and see the ghost footprints of our bed, our chairs.

'It's like a stage!' whispered Chris into the silence.

'Tap-dance! Tap-dance! Ra-ta-da-da!'

The downstairs neighbour banged the ceiling for me to stop.

Hammering on the door. I sat up in the dark, confused. As I opened the door it jerked against the security chain, pushed from the other side.

'They arrested Bob!'

'What?'

Mrs Sirussi was fully dressed, wearing her second-best wig, a shaggy black feather-cut like a busby. I pulled my dressing gown tighter.

'It's the middle of the night!' said Chris, behind me.

'They arrested Bob,' I told him. Mrs Sirussi tugged at my sleeve:

'Come! There's Police downstairs! They want to talk to you!'

Bob's apartment was already familiar to me, but I sensed Chris recoiling. Two monolithic policemen were searching the rooms: a young officer poking a stick into the bath, an older one making notes on a pad. Their uniforms, close up, were of thick, stiff cloth; navy-blue exoskeletons with snug guns on the wrinkled hips. They looked up as we came in.

'Français? English?' asked the older officer.

'Uh – English.'

'Do you know the man who lives here?'

'Only in passing.' Until that morning we had never exchanged a word.

'He has your name here.' He waved a piece of paper; it was our advert, with Bob's cloven-hoofed scrawl across the back. 'It says he owes you money. What's that about?'

'Oh, right! Yeah, he's going to buy some of our furniture . . . he *was*. What's happened?'

The two policemen looked at each other, unwilling to answer, but Mrs Sirussi interjected:

'He beat up Therese!' She seemed upset, probably aware now of the close shave she'd had with Bob.

'He assaulted his estranged partner,' corrected the older officer.

'You know his wife's name?' I asked Mrs Sirussi.

'Sure I do! See, Therese is in the bar, and Bob comes over . . .'

'The assailant approached his estranged partner . . .'

'And she starts beaking off to him about the kid . . .'

'The assailant engaged in an altercation with . . .'

'And then *these* guys get involved . . .'

'You can't say "assailant",' said the younger cop.

'Sure I can . . .'

'No, it's "the accused" . . .'

' "Accused", nothing! He took a swing at me himself . . .'

'Yeah, but until he's charged officially . . .'

'Look, who's writing this report? Go and check on the car, will ya?'

'Oh, right, pull rank on me!' The younger policeman stamped out in a huff. The older man closed his notebook, pushed his pen back into his top pocket.

'Ho-kay. Thanks for your co-operation. We know where you are if we need to ask anything else.'

In two days we would be back in Britain, gone forever, untraceable.

'Sure,' I said.

When the police had gone, Mrs Sirussi seemed to collapse. She sank into a dirty armchair, shook her head.

'What am I gonna do now!' Her voice had its usual sharp crackle, but she looked old and tiny, exhausted.

'I'll help you,' I said, touching her shoulder. 'We'll clean it up and you can rent it to someone really nice! At least he's gone now, hey?'

'You should have thrown him out ages ago,' said Chris.

'Yeah, you should have said you had a son who wanted the room, or something.'

Mrs Sirussi's eyes filled with tears. She struggled up out of the chair and turned her back so that we wouldn't see; wiped her forehead with a rough, scrubbing motion.

'Bob is my son,' she said, and began stripping the photographs from the wall. They tumbled in a heap at her feet, and twitched in the draught like broken wings as we closed the door.

The Thin Line

LYING IN BED, I can hear everything she does. It creeps into my dreams sometimes, the kind you get just before you wake, where you're watching, and in, a film, and

the robot has gone crazy, it strangles all the scientists with its spanner hands and starts to turn on the kitchen taps and the plumbing

rushes water through the house. She turns the tap off and the kettle toils through its stages, from the first sigh of the element to the plastic snap. I fall a hundred feet into my bed. The kitchen sounds shiver through the walls and floorboards, a direct line to my nerves. Gordon never notices but it always wakes me, sure as an alarm clock. He isn't here this morning. I planned this for when he was away.

I'm probably imagining that I can hear the feet of the kettle leaving the work surface, but there's a real rubber thump as they step back on, and then it's only two minutes to the microwave's humperdink kick – opening, closing, beep, hum, ting! Old people are supposed to know about making tea, but she hasn't got a scoobie. I tell her I like it four minutes, and she lies and says it was. And I've counted the teabags in the bin; she gets three cups out of one. She'd recycle them if she could. And then she microwaves it with the milk in, beyond the limits of human tolerance. It's her twentieth-century version of a cauldron.

I never hear her on the stairs. She must be able to fly, little jet packs in her slippers. She could surely come in at the window if she wanted.

For the past two months, our routine has been this:

Out of bed, nose to nose with my mother-in-law, I scream every time.

'Scared you, did I!'

'Aah!'

'Wakey wakey wakey/ Rise and shine!

Come and have your breakfast/ I've had mine!'

Any court in the land.

Then she'll give me the tea – handle towards me, her own hand cupped around the scalding china – and grab me in a Heimlich hug. It reminds me of a psychic surgeon I saw on television, working and digging his fingers into an abdomen, drawing out a dripping, spherical tumour, like a cricket ball that had been found in wet grass. I expect to see my mother-in-law holding my spleen in her hand one day.

Now there's the push, and she rattles the door handle. As a last resort, she knocks. I expected to feel some sense of occasion, but I'm relaxed, face down, tucking my toes under the mattress for maximum stretch. Fingers touching the seam on each side.

'Fiona?'

The sun comes through the curtains, bright and cool, an American movie: *woman in cotton nightie stretches and yawns. Everything so right that no good can come of it.*

'Fiona, there's something wrong with the door!'

Gordon wouldn't put a lock on; what if she was ill in the night? We'd never forgive ourselves.

I would.

Och, Fiona . . .

'Fiona, I'm spilling the tea!'

I have hammered a plank at the top and the bottom of the door. I did it last night. She was so pleased when I asked her to go out and check that the car lights were off, involving her. *Two women keeping house together, one young, one old. But all is not what it seems.* I parked it down the road to give myself a good ten minutes. Hammer hammer hammer. Quick!

* * *

Gordon's last morning onshore. She can't leave us alone even then.

'You'll be wanting some bacon for your breakfast, son!'

She hugs him. He's still in bed, naked; the pressure of her fingers leaves fading red marks on his back.

'Aye.'

'And an egg.'

'Gordon,' I say.

'Just a wee eggie! You'll be needing your strength.' Her hand forms a 'c', a wrench, demonstrating the size of a very small egg indeed.

'Aye, thanks.'

He gives me a smile and shrug: *I know*! But he still gets his egg.

'Don't be long!'

I hold my breath until she is clattering again in the kitchen.

'She'll catch us at it one day!'

'She'll *nae*!' Grumpy. The doctor has told us to give it a rest sometimes, saving up our fragile fertility, hoping it will coincide once it's not so knackered. Which means, for some reason, that I am responsible for the word 'No'.

'Gordon! *No*! I don't know how you can do it with her in the house anyway!'

But it seems to goad him on. I worry about the home life; perhaps she caught him with a porn mag as a kid. The formative age. At night I can hear her in the room next door. She reads (fat romances from the library). She breathes. She *prays*, weight flattening the mattress, then a sigh. *Thank God for my bed!*

'Gordon, she'll hear us! When is she going home, anyway?'

'When her roof's done.'

'When's that going to be?'

'Och, they're dragging their feet a bit. I'll have a word with them.'

'No, *I'll* have a word with them. I'll go round and take their ladder away until they're finished.'

He laughs because he thinks I don't mean it; but I do, I think it right through, up to the point where they'd all have to be on the roof at the same time for it to work.

'Fiona!'

Tea down on the landing, a circular scrape. She tries the bathroom door, but I nailed that too; the rooms are connected. Back to the bedroom. Jurassic Park; *the dinosaur snuffs at the door, hot breath.*

'Fiona!'

I haven't really thought it out this far, whether it is all right to answer.

'What?' My voice weak as tea. '*What*!'

Now she knows I'm here. Temper rising.

'Your tea's getting cold!' She tries the door again. 'Come on, you'll be late!'

Then she goes quiet, but I know she's still there. She's waiting me out. *They're cunning beasts, dammit – almost human intelligence! Movie sweat on faces. Jungle sounds and a night filter on the camera.*

Years ago, sitting with my friends after school, a regular topic:

'Which room in your house would you choose to be locked in?'

'To keep out the robbers!'

'The kidnappers!'

Angela's house had a downstairs toilet, so she always chose the kitchen. You would need to secure two doors. I always chose the bathroom. Just one door.

'The immersion heater would keep you warm, and there's the bath and the toilet and the taps.'

'You wouldn't have any electrics.'

'What would you eat?'

I have packet soups, a travel kettle, UHT milk, and things in tins that I can eat cold. Ryvita and Ribena. A tin opener, of course. I bought them in front of her, bold, said it was in case of a power cut ('Good girl!', crush crush). I hard-boiled six eggs, not wee eggs, muckle great eggs. They should keep for a few days like that, me not having a fridge. Dried potato mash, as eaten by astronauts and aliens. Books, lovely books, and a CD player, with a selection of CDs, that I brought through from the living room. I also have a plastic wand from the chemist that I *didn't* buy in front of her. Later on, I will have to try and pee on it. That's entertainment!

She stamps on the landing, making out that she's been away and is coming back. Like, if she does that, she can start the morning again and it'll be ordinary.

Usually, she lays out my work uniform while I'm in the shower. It's spread on the bed when I come out, like a page from a dress-a-dolly book. She even chooses my underwear.

'Really, you don't have to.'

'Just a bitty help! You don't want to be late for work, do you?'

'Frankly, my dear – '

But she'll be poking around in the bathroom, spreading out the shower curtain to dry like cormorants' wings.

'Fine to have an ensuite bathroom!' she yells. 'Gordon's spoiling you!'

'It's fine and private.'

No answer.

'I said, it's nice to have a bit of privacy!'

She comes back in and folds my nightdress. 'It's not ower warm this . . . right! I'll go and make you some sandwiches. Fourteen minutes!'

Yesterday, I wrote NAFF OFF on the cardboard from a pack of tights and put it on top of the underwear in my drawer.

The friction of her feet on the landing carpet.

'I found your note,' she says sourly. 'If you don't want me going in your drawer you only have to say.'

I jump out of the bed and press my face to the door.

'I don't want you going in my drawer!'

The paint is cold on my cheek, immobilising it, muffling my voice.

She huffs a bit, then she really does go, but she's back in a minute, panicking.

'Someone's stolen the CD machine!'

'It's in here!'

I put on the first CD that I chose for the occasion: *Powermad. Slaughterhouse. I'm Laura Dern, I'm Lula, dancing on the bed in a hail of cotton-wool balls.*

'Well, I'm phoning Gordon!' she says.

She'll be lucky. I've got the phone in here too.

Gordon rearranges the CDs when he's back onshore. It's the first thing he does, hands trembling from the homecoming hangover. He arranges them alphabetically, or by era, or by genre. Then he plays golf.

'Let me come with you!'

'Ah, Fiona, it's boring.'

'*You* go!'

'You'd have nothing to do.'

'I would, I'd bring a book. Gordon, please, I just want to be away from *her* for a bit.'

'She'd come with you.'

'You could tell her.'

'Look, Fi.' Hands on my shoulders. '*I* want to be on my own too. Just a wee whiley. You can go swimming or something. She won't want to go there.'

'Isn't this a nice little run!'

'Don't hug me when I'm driving!'

'This is *nice*! Just the two of us. It'll do Gordon good to be away from our blethering!'

I make a point of not speaking until we're at the pool.

The changing room is the only solitude I've had for, God, two months. Two months! Her roof'll be like the Taj Mahal. My pants peel off inside my jeans, a little stowaway turban with a Marks and Spencer label. Naked, I am protected, I am properly alone. No-one looks at you naked; or, if their eyes are turned in your direction, they put on an expression that shows they're not really focusing. Into the black Lycra, and they can look again. I have a serious swimsuit, a swimmer's suit, no leopard-skin bikini with bits flopping over the top. But I swim like I'm towing bricks. It doesn't matter. The chlorine smell is timelessly exciting, coaxing me in.

Actually, it smells like our bathroom does now, since she took to bleaching the toilet, pushing my organic cleaners to the back of the cupboard. She doesn't reckon they do the job.

'But they're better for the planet!'

'The *planet*?' She can't think which planet I mean.

Some things are different. They don't make you skip through the verruca bath these days. And they heat the water more, so I can slip in easily. I look down at the ripples moving from my body; the water behaves as it does for the good swimmers, encouraging. Even without my contact lenses, I can see her in the spectators' gallery, wagging her head like some kind of lizard that's bored in its tank. I ignore her and set out, turtling my neck to keep my face above the water.

Labouring towards the deep end, hogging the wall, I'm going away from her. The speed swimmers barge me aside, terrify me, but I'm Going Away. Swimming back, I'm aware of her white face pressed to the window, the cerise lipstick in a concerned 'o'. Some girl on the make-up counter having a laugh. My suit drags, netting water; I've lost weight. I feel her eyes on me, as tight as the rubber band on my ankle. It used to fit on my wrist. At the shallow end, I make an elaborate turn and send a little kid in arm bands bobbing like a buoy. His mother makes a bay of her arms; he swims in, out again, daring. She chases him, stalking in the water like the Ed 90 in *Robocop – You have three seconds to comply*! I kick hard and swim away.

I've never stayed in this long before. I swim until I'm weak, until my stomach is a taut, tired scoop of muscle, until the lifeguard has to tell me twice to get out, and blows his whistle at me. I haul myself shaking on to the tiles and scowl at him.

She grabs me while I'm towelling my hair.

'Jesus!'

'Naughty girl!'

'How did you, I mean, what – '

'I had a little word; they let me in!'

She does this, she talks to people, gets special dispensation. There's a hot chocolate moustache drying on her upper lip. She isn't put off by my nakedness.

'Ooh, you're getting thin, aren't you?' She pinches a chicken wing from my hip.

'Ow!'

'You should be careful; some of those lady athletes can't have babies.'

I buy a packet of tampons from the machine to annoy her. They only ever sell the massive ones, like sheep wearing leads; the ones you expect to absorb all your bodily fluids and leave you as a pile of salt. I'll never use them, they'll stay in my handbag, turning grey and ratty.

In the mirror on the way out, she looks rosy and happy. I look shocked and white, browless, like Elizabeth the First. It's funny how you always look like crap after a swim; it's supposed to be healthy.

Later, I am sick. The broth she made comes back unchewed, pearl barley and globs of fat. She's not exactly Granny Baxter. The chlorine leaps fresh to my skin, my face glows and my eyes are bright. Funny how you always look great after you've thrown up. It's a better work out than swimming, better than a good cry.

'Very clever, taking the phone! What if there's an emergency?'

I don't reply, I just roll a boiled egg against the door to crack the shell. Let her figure that one out.

The eggs were a mistake, though. I've already shifted two, and the smell of this one is something medieval, makes me feel sick. And I've brought so many books that I don't know which to read first.

A wooden clip-clop on the landing.

'I've got a chair up by the door! I'm going to sit here until you come out!'

'Go on then!'

In, out, in, out. She breathes like other people snore, moist and trollish, water running down the walls. She coughs; someone dropping a manhole cover.

'Did you remember to take your pill?'

'My pill?'

I miss it, I miss the routine of pushing the white kernel through the green foil each morning, like a seed pod bursting; poor analogy in the circumstances. I don't know what she's –

'What are you talking about?'

'Your pill. Your Prozac.'

'It's not *Prozac*!'

She picks these things up from the television, from the scare stories in her magazines. If what she reads is anything to go by, the whole purpose of Prozac is to turn you *into* a psychotic. They only give it to Tragic Mums.

'They're not Prozac; they're just a, a mild anti-depressant! Not everything is Prozac! And besides, I've stopped taking them.' I go to the bathroom. I come out again. 'And besides, how do *you* know?'

I go back to the bathroom. I check my watch and open the packet from the chemist. The stick is sealed in plastic, it has a cap that you remove to get at the tip. The colours are a non-committal combination of clinical and hopeful, blue and white, as neutral as Switzerland. It must be a hard product to advertise; you can't rely on your consumer base (females of childbearing age) wanting a particular outcome. A positive result could be a negative thing, or vice versa. So the model in the advert always has an indistinct expression, they make great use of the shoulders and hair. Soft focus. Nothing to indicate that she's just peed on a stick. All the other cruddy things that women have to contend with, and they choose to gloss over that.

It's not easy to do. I get most of it on my hand.

But the hard part is the waiting.

I re-read the instructions until I have totally confused myself.

And I wait for the thin line.

* * *

I'm watching Gordon when I get the idea for the planks.

Let me rephrase that.

A week onshore and even he has played enough golf. He's on to the chores now, in this case the garden fence, treating it with something that Does What It Says On The Can. Some of the slats are too old, and he prises them off with the claw of the hammer, nails new ones on. It's a sunny day, and I want to be outside, helping him. I used to help my dad when I was little, and creosote is like Proust's madeleines to me. But the neighbourhood kids have got involved, and he would rather trust the holding of nails to a seven-year-old who can't co-ordinate the wiping of his own nose.

She brings out endless mugs of tea.

'It's more thirst-quenching than a cold drink!'

The microwave is working overtime; the tea is steaming even on this hot day.

'That's a fine job you're doing, son!'

'He won't let me help him.'

'Oh, you don't want to strain yourself in your condition.'

I stare at her.

'What condition? I'm not *in* a condition!'

'Ah, but any day now, eh? Just do what the doctor says.'

Gordon harrumphs and bends to inspect the fence.

'Gordon!' We haven't said anything to her; we'd agreed to keep it a secret until we knew. 'Have you been listening at doors?' I'm shouting at her. 'Have you?'

'Now now . . .'

Gordon mutters something.

'What was that, Gordon?'

'Uh, I sort of . . . said something.'

'Did you! *Said* something! Did you now!'

And maybe we could have worked it out, but she got involved.

'It was just to prepare me – you know, you'll be needing a bitty help. I can come back and stay any time, I don't mind. Come on Fiona – it'll be lovely. A wee family! All my chicks around me!'

Gordon's last night. I sleep badly, the hammer and planks under my side of the mattress. When he has gone, I stash the food in the wardrobe, dig out the travel kettle, jumpy as a thief in my own house.

The next night, hammering in the planks, I am exhilarated.

Now I am calm. I stare at the stick until I am sure, then I put it in the bin. I go through to the bedroom, take up the hammer, and start clawing off the planks.

Sumo

'SUMO!'
'Shut up.'

'Sumo-oh!'

A killer look, a disdainful silence. We both glance at my mother for her reaction, but she is frying up another round of eggy bread.

'Sumo' (whispered). 'Sumosumosumo. Blobby Sumo wrestler.'

I study the kitchen window, feign fascination in the dead flies behind the radio. Years of cream paint have softened the lines of the windowsill, and there is a solid trickle of gloss down the side of the electric socket. It's one of the old, round-pin kind, with a tower of adaptors coupled to it. I count the slats of the Venetian blind, concentrate on the fingerprints that someone has wiped in their dust, but a prickling has started behind my eyes and the next time my brother calls me 'Sumo' . . .

'Mam! She kicked me! Owie owie owie!'

'He keeps calling me "Sumo"!'

My sister holds her spoon aloft like the girl on the cereal box, grinning, waiting for the next development. She is always stalwartly on the side of whoever is winning. As my mother gazes fondly at my brother – the little man, the pride and joy – I know I have lost. Where my brother is concerned, my mother is a bent judge.

She passes sentence: 'Oh, leave him alone! He's younger than you.' Playing to the gallery, she adds, 'Now eat your breakfast, Sumo.'

A red tide of anger rises up in me, jerks me from my chair like a puppet, and I watch as if from a distance as I fling a brown arc of Weetabix across everyone in the kitchen. Then there is chair throwing, toast flying like *shuriken*, until I feel my mother's small hands at the waistband of my shorts.

'Run!' she shouts. 'Run like hell! I can't hold her for long!'

They bolt, screeching and baying, through the kitchen door and up the garden path. I whirl and twist, frantic, and my mother doesn't know how close I have come to biting her when she finally loses her grip and releases me like an arrow.

My brother has been calling me 'Sumo' since I got my first training bra. It's part of the way my body has been playing tricks on me lately; thrilling me with possibilities, or shaking me awake with worries in the night. A book called *Growing Up is Fun!* appeared one day on my bed, and I pretend that I don't pore over it, tracking my own progress against it. Its brisk, cheerful tone can't console me for the fact that I am becoming horrible, literally by the book. My thighs have begun to pucker like citrus peel. My forehead, when pressed to the page of a book, leaves a transparent grease mark. And, although I was the last in my class, my periods have finally started.

My first period arrived while my aunties and uncles were visiting. I'd had a bad stomach all day, and I was offering a plate of Marks and Spencers' Fondant Fancies to my Uncle Dai when I felt something wrong, a definite lurch, a change. My Uncle Dai dithered over choosing, wanting the chocolate one, naturally; wanting *both* the chocolate ones if he was being honest. But still he made magicians' passes over the lemon and the pink, pretending they were equally desirable so that no-one would mind when he left them. The aunties watched him fondly; they thought he was entitled to the chocolate anyway. I clenched my knees together and willed him to get on with it, to make his greedy choice.

'Well, now . . .' he said.

When my mother found out why I had thrown the Fondant Fancies at Uncle Dai, she got the packet of Things from the airing cupboard. The Things had been hidden there for three years, miniature stretchers in coy floral wrapping, but all I had done until then was read and re-read the frightening instruction leaflet. It didn't square with the book's suggestion that I would want to play tennis, ride a horse, or simply wander around holding a single flower.

The dog yaps his excitement as I run past his pen and smash the gate open. Our garden backs on to a wood; it's not large, but there is a playground, and a quarry that is so sternly forbidden that we feel compelled to play there. In the summer, the wood is filled with ferns, shoulder high; you would only need to crouch to stay hidden there until autumn, waiting while the bright, moist green turned to fox-coloured bracken and lost its sap smell.

They have to be there somewhere.

I turn methodical, lobbing rocks into the undergrowth in a grid pattern. It's like Battleships: B2 – miss. B3 – miss. Then it's B4 – hit! and my sister leaps up, yelling. They're too far away to catch, but I follow their flight at a regular pace, conserving my energy for the killer sprint to come. They crest the hill, heading for the playground, and I stop to pull a branch from a birch tree. It loses me time, but it buys me a weapon. I hold it like a rifle against my chest; it feels good and serious, and it stops my breasts from jumping.

A few months ago, my mother saw me running down the garden path and decided it was time to take me to Renée Gwilym's, the bra shop in Neath. As it was my first time, Madame Gwilym herself took a tape with cold metal ends from around her neck and gave me what felt like a public measuring. She and my mother went into a learned, arcane huddle, and I came out furnished with the bra equivalent of National Health spectacles – the same colour pink, too. I thought it was pretty cool once I'd got it home and posed about in the mirror for a while. I even kept the box; it had a picture on the front of an unblemished teenage girl modelling the white version for all to see. I wondered how she felt, being on a box all over the country, when I had almost blushed to death just carrying it home in a brown paper bag.

They're waiting for me in the playground, perched like rooks at the top of the slide. I circle them slowly, turning on my best death stare, but it feels ridiculous when they're so high above me. On each pass I make, the sun shines off the business end of the slide, dazzling me, which certainly won't do. I take myself to the swings and hang from the chains, turning nonchalant somersaults. This, at least, I can still do, though the danger of cracking my head increases with each spate of my growth.

The birch branch shows its age with each gnarled knuckle along its length. In my case, it's the shoes going up a size with every visit to Clark's. My mother grizzles at each new version of my school uniform, as if I am growing on purpose to bankrupt her. It's sweet when my sister has to wear my old skirts to school; she hates it.

She calls to me from the top of the slide:

'Hey, Sumo! Don't break the swings!'

But I am the cool one, I am the queen of restraint, and she will get bored before I do. She can't even spit on me from that distance; each shining glob falls just short. She makes a final effort, then sighs and shrugs.

Then she pushes my brother off the slide.

'Bitch!' he shouts at her, at me, and at all treacherous sister-kind before he is delivered neatly into my arms. I grab him, propel him off the slide, and rub his face in the dirt, shouting 'Weight advantage! Weight advantage!' He struggles and squalls, but I press him down with my foot and set about thrashing him with the birch branch. I do a good job, thorough and merciless. On Monday, I will tell everyone that he got kicked in by a girl.

Then I become aware that we are being watched.

Wendy Owen is in the playground.

Wendy Owen is in my class at school, but she is distinctly out of my class too. She started her periods in primary school. She wears gorgeous, lacy bras under her shirt at gym and, while everyone else wears white aertex, she has a red, plunging T-shirt. She has a father in a wheelchair who has to take medicine and who spends all day throwing darts at pictures of soccer players, but she still manages to be more normal than me. And Wendy has *boyfriends.* Today's boyfriend is called Barry, it says so on his knuckles. Each one bears a home-tattooed letter, with the 'Y' on the thumb. He stands beside her, gangly and thin in his bomber jacket; covered in acne, shorter than Wendy, and thrillingly male.

Wendy is wearing a denim jacket and high-heeled shoes and she is definitely, definitely wearing one of her lovely bras. She has make-up on straight out of a *Jackie* magazine article: 'How to Look Fanciable for Fellas'. The heels are a ridiculous thing to wear for a walk in the woods, and I wish I had a pair; my T-shirt is all pulled up where my mother restrained me and one of my trainers is suspiciously brown.

'Are you out playing?' Wendy snickers.

'Nah, just jogging,' I say, trying to make it sound mature. 'My brother fell down. You all right now, Ger?' He makes violent gestures, demonstrating silently what he would like to do to me, and limps away.

'Ri-ight.' Wendy isn't fooled. 'We're out courting,' she says, and drags Barry's limp arm around her waist, exposing the words 'Man U' above his bony wrist. He obediently starts hoovering her face with his thick, red lips, still holding his cigarette in his free hand, so it must be horrible to kiss him. Like an ashtray, the school nurse said. Still. I wonder what it would be like to kiss a boy. Nothing like a pillow, I bet. A bit like your hand but wetter.

I wait for them to stop. I keep waiting, and then I say:

'Well, I'd better get going!' But they don't listen to me. They are Lost in Love. 'See ya,' I add and Wendy's muffled voice, buried in Barry's face, says:

'Smmeeyah.'

I go to the quarry. It's always quiet there, except that one time I saw a tramp eating a sandwich, so now I go carefully, ready to run.

I read an article about deer-stalking in my dad's *Shooting Times* magazine. It said you should walk on the outsides of your feet to avoid making a noise, so that's what I do. At the top of the quarry I crouch and peep over the edge. Thirty feet below, my brother and sister are making a fort out of all the rubbish that's been thrown there, threading branches through the milk-crates and shopping trolleys to make it tight. They're engrossed, and my mouth turns dry with the possibilities.

I circle the quarry until I'm above and behind them, then I climb down, unclenching every muscle slowly so that I almost trickle down the rock face. The saplings support me. I take them so gently in my hand that they don't know I'm doing it; release them so carefully that they don't spring back. I choose the footholds with the most moss, mould my profile to the rock. My fingers reach into cold crevices the texture of toads, finding damp, wedged sticks. The stone outside is dry, pale grey and sun-warmed, scarred with spray paint and marker pen. Jinksy woz 'ere, and Rachel luvs Barry; wait until Wendy finds out. S.C.F.C., Neath Boys Rule. I'm getting closer, I can hear my sister talking.

'Give us it, Geraint. I'll stick it here. If she tries to jump round the side she'll hit this spike.'

I hold my breath, then let it out in molecules.

Our Biology teacher said that cavemen were the hunters, but that cavewomen were just gatherers, and then he made a joke about his wife going shopping; but I feel a hunter's instinct now, watching, judging, planning my attack. From the size of the barrier they're building, they must be really scared of me. Perfect, I can use that. I'm at ground level now, in the undergrowth. It would be so easy to rush them, but they'd hear me, they'd escape. Self control. Self control. I move to the rhythm of my own quiet breathing. I pick up a fallen branch; it takes an age. Self control. I could almost touch them, but I go for effect instead. The element of surprise. As my sister feels my breath on her neck, starts to turn, frowning, I scream as loud as I can. And I leap.

'AAAAARGH!'

'EEEEEEEEEEE!'

I get in a few good blows but then they manage to push through the barrier, milk-crates, dead wood and all. My sister rips her T-shirt, which means she will get a row later – result! I can't chase them far, I'm laughing too much, but I can hear them crashing through the woods. My sister is crying with fright; my brother is screaming uncontrollably.

I lie back on the quarry rocks to enjoy my triumph. I wriggle to a warmer spot and bask. The sun needles through the trees and shines red through my eyelids. I feel the tiny, sticky feet of a lizard running over my hand, and, like a benevolent god, I let him pass. It's good here. I can sense the trembling of every animal that watches me from the bushes. This place must be amazing at night. Rabbits, foxes . . . more rabbits. Owls. Yeah, owls! I'm in touch with Nature. Wendy can keep her stupid boyfriend.

Something brushes my leg, and I open my eyes. I think I have slept; my mouth is dry. Something else lands not far off, bounces on the turf, but I don't see what it is, then suddenly, on my stomach, there is

a dead snake.

I *think* it's dead . . .

Bolting upright, I scatter spiders and beetles, the Lilliput insects that crept into my hair while I slept. The place where the snake fell feels like an imprint: a curl of disgust branded on my stomach. It lies at my feet, gnarled and dry; its eyes glazed with dust. They must have found it and thrown it down on me when they saw I was asleep. I rage at myself for dropping my guard, and dodge the scatter of stones that they kick down as they run from the top of the quarry.

I could say they threw a snake at me.

I could say they were at the quarry (but so was I).

I could say anything, and my mother would still side with them.

But none of this matters as I have just thought of a way to get back at them.

Llew-next-door works in the slaughterhouse, though we have to call it the abattoir when he calls round. He conceals packets of Refreshers and Love Hearts in his sliced, battered hands and says:

'Even Stevens!', and we have to choose a hand to see which sweets we get. Llew brings round tripe and sheeps' heads from the slaughterhouse, too. They steam in buckets in the kitchen while Llew accepts a whisky, with the same surprise every time – 'Whisky? Aye, just a snifter, then.' Later, my father feeds the sheeps' heads to the dog.

Sometimes, when I can't sleep, I wrap my blanket around me and sit in the bedroom window watching Dad chop the sheeps' heads up. First he spreads an old newspaper on the garden step, and sometimes he crouches there for a while, reading it. Then he gets the cleaver from the coal shed and sharpens it with a long, metal steel. The local cats hear the shik-shik-shik; a constellation of yellow eyes appears through the dark, and they gather to slaver and mew on the garden wall. My dad lays the sheeps' heads on the step and with a swing of the cleaver CHOK! he splits the skulls. The cats creep warily, hungrily forward to eat the scraps from his bloodied hands. It helps me get off to sleep.

I cut through next-door's garden to avoid disturbing the dog. At the coal-house door I lift the latch, covering it with my hand to mask the noise, and close the door gently behind me. The door has holes and broken planks in it; I close my eyes for a moment, then open them, and there is enough light to see by.

I root out some old newspapers, kept there for firelighting and skull chopping, and I spread some of them on the coal to sit on. I keep the others aside to read while I wait. I listen to my mother in the house; clanking the washing up, singing along badly to the radio, guessing the words to Italian arias. Now and then I look through one of the holes, keeping my eyes accustomed to the light because I don't want to make my attack half-blinded. There is a danger, too, of going off the boil if your enemy keeps you waiting. You have to keep your instincts sharp, like when you're following someone; you have to be afraid they'll hear you, otherwise you get careless and they do. I make myself think of the snake flopping down on me, recall how I felt when I pelted them with the breakfast. I think of my mother saying, 'Oh, you're just too sensitive; ignore them, can't you?', and I get a great lump in my throat, swallow it down. I test the cleaver on one of the newspapers; it falls into strips.

The dog starts barking at the top of the garden and I hear the garden gate slam. Knowing they're back gives me my edge again. I get on to my feet and crouch there, bouncing slightly, preparing myself for action. I can hear their voices as they come down the path.

'Well, I'm telling Mam.'

'Well, I'm telling her first!' and the slap-slap of my sister's trainers. She's cocky now. The sound of their footsteps changes from path to steps, four feet away. Three. Two.

I step out of the coal shed.

The scene has a vibrant, viewfinder clarity.

My brother's amazed face. My sister, open-mouthed behind him. My mother bustling out of the kitchen, stopping as if she has walked into glass.

The sunlight on the blade as it seems to hover in the warm air.

Power Cuts

THE KITCHEN HAD a caravan feel, primitive and under-equipped despite its size. My mother was washing up with brisk care, a dishcloth slung over her shoulder. She observed that it was some bloody holiday for her.

My father sat potching at the table. With a precise movement, he drove a fish hook into his thumb.

'Blimey – flipping – Charlie!'

He sat like a big-eyed good boy for me to pull it out, then he sucked at the wound, examined it.

'Dad, no wonder,' I said, 'you've got hands like a mole.'

He laid them on the table, slabby-flat, and looked at them as if for the first time, blinking in the poor light from the standard lamp. I held out my own.

'Never mind, then; so have I.' But he hadn't taken it as an insult; it was just something.

My brother-in-law came downstairs, made an arrival of it. He flicked on the fluorescent light and posed in the kitchen with a fishing bag, waders, a rod, pointing at them in turn:

'My dad lent it me. Bought them last week. Borrowed it off Nigel.'

He had a hat with fishing flies hooked into it. If he banged his head, I thought, they would scrape his skull. He would hear them wherever he went: 'skrit skrit'. It would drive him mental.

* * *

Renting the cottage had been his idea.

'Yes, of course; it's more practical,' I agreed on the phone, although I had planned a family reunion at my own home: long breakfasts around the kitchen table, talking over coffee into the night. Somehow I hadn't imagined my brother-in-law there at all. But in the two years since I had come to Aberdeen, he seemed to have taken over as the head of the family. The Alpha Male. They were more afraid now of upsetting him than upsetting me.

My sister stirred coffee in a Pyrex jug, poured it into a tartan Thermos flask, and screwed the top on double-tight. Her husband turned for her to tuck it into his fishing bag.

'Come on, Will!' he said to my father, 'The little fishes will all be in bed!'

My sister and mother remained standing, knowing that to sit down would be seen as a lack of encouragement. The men fussed and cluttered over getting ready, the self-important centre of the night-fishing Universe, and when they finally left they reeled the noise out of the room with them.

We stood motionless for a moment, letting the quiet build, enjoying it.

'You can almost hear the silence!' whispered my mother, which broke the spell and sent us scurrying for a corkscrew and glasses. My mother pirouetted, laughing, shaking a bottle of wine like a maraca, and we danced a wild conga out of the kitchen.

The living room of the cottage was decorated in horror-hunting style: stuffed animals, gnarled and snarling in glass boxes; framed maps of the River Dee, brown and speckled as trout. My sister was on a Diet Coke jag, so I poured the wine into two mismatched tumblers for my mother and myself, and we sat back and toasted each other:

'To the holidays!'

'Here's to the Girls' Night In!'

When I was little and followed my father around, I would watch him feed the dogs, amazed and frightened by the violence of their greed. Steel dishes rang, and Dad would stand cursing in the middle, seeing fair play with a word or a blow as they choked covetously at their food. Feeding the cat, by contrast, was a tea-ceremony of politeness, right down to the blue china bowl.

Now we sat neatly, curled like kittens on the threadbare sofas. With a flourish, my mother took three Walnut Whips from her handbag. She had hidden them there until the men had gone, knowing that they wouldn't understand the ritual: unfolding the wrappers in unison, snapping the walnuts off for our mother, who liked their bitterness, and biting the tops off like torturers. We delved with our tongues into the acid-sweet foam, got the chocolate on our faces and smirked at each other. I had grown out of the childhood treat, the sickly taste, but that wasn't the point. It was the bonding, the being together that mattered.

'Mnnmnmn! Miss Piggy!' said my mother, and sighed. I looked at the stuffed animals, the dust on their eyes, and blinked hard.

'Why don't people stuff fish?' I said.

'They do!'

'They don't!'

'Well . . . swordfish and things they do. And sharks.'

'Oh. Do they put them in an action pose, then, or do they just stuff them stiff?'

'They stuff them . . . with breadcrumbs!'

My sister drained her glass with both hands, child-like.

'How would you stuff an eel then?'

'An eeeel!'

'With a pool cue, for sure.'

My mother, her hand raised solemnly, swore that what she really wanted for her birthday was a stuffed eel, and that if either of us had a daughter's love for her, then that was what we'd get her.

'All right, then,' I said, 'But I'm not wrapping it for you.'

'I'm not fussy. Just put a bow round its neck.'

'Yeah, but, Mam, how will she send it from Aberdeen to Neath? It would snap.'

'I'll send it in a welly.' I mimed a postwoman knocking at the door. 'Eel in a welly for Mrs Griffiths. Could you sign for it, please?'

Since she arrived, my mother had been comparing Scotland to Wales. Each morning she looked out to the Hill of Fare, to the bruised indigo of the mountains beyond, and drew back like a snail pulling in its horns.

'It's too big! You could get lost just looking!'

'Oh, but it's lovely when you're out there,' I said. 'You see pheasants and grouse and – '

'Beardy Americans with rucksacks!' she said.

'Oh, shush! And there's salmon – '

'No there's not,' said my father. 'We'd have caught some if there were.'

I frowned at him. I had wanted them to fall for Aberdeen the way that I had. So, while the men spent their days fishing, I marched my mother and sister along Union Street until they mewed for a cup of tea and a sit down. I pointed out every Westie and every kilt. I drove them out to a field where I knew there was a Highland cow and watched him nodding carefully as they fed him cheese sandwiches. Finally I took them to the Brig o' Balgownie, where my sister scampered around with a camera, climbing into people's gardens for the best angles.

'So you're not coming back to Wales then?' asked my mother, slyly casual. 'There's a new Marks and Spencers outside Cardiff now, mind.'

'It's nice here,' I said evasively.

'Are you going to stay?'

I thought of an old lady, of a type I had learnt to call a 'wifie', who had taken my arm on the bus and told me about Aberdeen.

'I've seen 'em come and I've seen 'em go,' she said. 'But mostly I've seen 'em go.'

It had felt like a challenge. I wanted to be one of the ones who didn't go.

'Dunno,' I told my mother, scuffing the toe of my shoe, twelve years old again.

She looked seriously into my face.

'Tell me, Sara, have you tried haggis?'

She made it sound worse than heroin.

The dusty old sofas seemed to have been thrown rather than arranged around the cottage walls, like furniture in the Wall of Death. My sister sat plastered into one of them as if by gravity, her eyelids fluttering. She yawned, and I envied the beautiful, blue-blooded vein that showed through on her jawline.

'Flagging, Meg?'

'A bit. I'm staying up, though,' and she fell asleep. My mother nudged me and pointed.

'Aaaw!' we said.

'She's been a bit out of it all trip.'

'I don't think she's well.' My mother loved to entertain dark thoughts.

'Nah, she's always needed her sleep like that.' I stretched. 'Remember when . . .' but my sentence trailed off as all the lights in the cottage fell away and I could see nothing. The darkness seemed to buzz in my ears and I heard my own voice, small and high,

'Mam! What happened?'

'Waah!' she answered, then 'Power cut!' She sounded far away.

'Oh! Oh God! Ha. Ha ha. Where are you?'

'I don't know!'

I forced myself not to panic at the sudden loss of vision. *Cool head. Find the curtains, open the curtains.*

'Mam?'

'Oooh!'

She was standing in the corner with a cushion on her head.

'Don't worry; I've got a torch in the car. Hold on.'

Sitting in the driver's seat I felt more confident. I found the torch in the glovebox and flicked the switch through the functions: amber, red, fluorescent and flashing. Far too elaborate, but I was glad of it now.

Back in the house I said, 'Don't worry, we can have a disco! Look.'

The two of them rushed me for control of the torch.

I fended them off and we organised a search for candles. We found a bundle under the sink, clacking waxily against each other, and two holders with glass covers in a box marked 'PoweR Cut's'.

'Look at that! It must happen all the time.'

'What a rip-off!'

'The joys of country living.'

I lit two candles for the holders, manoeuvred the covers on and felt the glass turn warm under my fingers. Our faces flickered, dripping with shadows.

'Hey, we're a coven!'

'Let's go and look at the stuffed animals now!'

'Let's not, Mam, okay?'

'Oh-kay.'

'So. What are we going to do now, then?'

The best thing would be to go to bed,' murmured Megan, dormouse-quiet.

We decided to sleep in my mother's bed, the largest, at least until the men got back.

'We're still managing without them, though.'

'Yeah! This is just to keep warm.'

'Let them sleep on the sofa!'

'Yeah!'

The bed sheets were cold and heavy. We scrambled about to get warm, a tangle and slap of legs, and I got the bottom end, shuggled my face into a solid feather pillow. My mother hinted, 'I can't remember when I last had a foot rub', so I obliged until Meg said,

'Uh, thanks, but those are my feet.'

We started to giggle. My mother kicked me, and I grabbed her ankles and shook her, cackling:

'I will now initiate you into the mysteries of – Scottish Country Dancing!'

'Argh! Gerroff! Help me, Meg!'

They beaned me with the pillows until I fell out, cracked my knee on the floor, lay there laughing and groaning.

'So,' said my mother, 'What shall we sing?'

I scrambled back in, pulled up the covers.

' "*Counting the Goats*?" ' I said.

'I can't remember it.'

' "*Sosban Fach*!" '

'Wha-at? That's a Llanelli song! The old enemy! Shame on you for not remembering that.'

' "*Y Mae Afon*", then,' I said. 'I'll do the alto. One two three – *Y mae afon, ei frydiau y lawen hant* (is that right?), *Y lawen ha-ant* (I'll do the alto), *ddinas Duw* (dammit, Mam, *I'll* do the alto!) . . .'

'All right then,' she interrupted, 'Here's one!' She put on a husky drawl.

'*See what the boys in the back room will have, and tell them I'm having the same*! Thank you, Miss Marlene Dietrich!' She applauded herself.

'Well if you're just going to be silly . . .'

'Haven't you learnt any songs since you came to Scotland?' she said.

I thought. 'Er – *I'm a fire starter, twisted fire starter*!'

'Scottish songs, I meant!'

'Oh! I know! Remember music lessons in school, Meg? "*Skye Boat Song*"?' She didn't answer. 'I'll start you off,' I said.

'*Speed, bonny boat, like a bird on the wing, Onward, the sailors cry, Carry the lad who is born to be king Over the sea to – the sea* – Meg? Meg, are you crying?'

I sat up. My sister took a breath and started to weep in earnest.

'Oh, *cariad*, what's wrong?' cried Mam, and we all reached for each other in the dark. My sister sat upright and sobbed, and we enfolded her, sat rocking until we seemed like one being. I felt puzzled and angry and inexplicably guilty, my own throat straining in sympathy.

'I'm all right,' Megan managed at last. 'But I think I'm pregnant.'

There was a silence.

And then my sister laugh-cried. 'I'm all right!' she said again, reassuring us now. 'I'm happy and everything, I'm only crying because it's so – so – o mu – uch!' She sniffed, a bubbling, snurfing sound, and I dug under the pillow for a tissue.

Sitting up a tree. The mushroom smell of moss in the rain, sticking to the knees of our jeans. We wore matching tank tops, and flares that wouldn't tuck into our wellies; my wellies were black, hers were red.

'I'm never going to have babies,' she said.

'Ugh, no! Imagine all that mess!'

'Babies smell.'

She didn't even have a baby doll. My gran had bought her one once, and she had tortured it with red pen and dismemberment. Its body still swung from the ladder in our neighbour's shed; naked, garrotted with wool, its eyes poked out. And our neighbour was a Chapel man. We were going to catch it when he found out; my dad would have to go round and apologise.

A rabbit hopped out under the tree and she leaned forward and spat on it. A direct hit.

'I'm going to be a grandmother!' said Mam.

'I'm going to be a mother,' corrected my sister, jealous of her position already.

A baby! It was another thing I hadn't been there for, this decision to procreate. To become grown up. My sister spoke practically, of maternity leave and birth dates. I thought of biblical dynasties and Biology lessons and Babygros. My little sister. A pregnant woman. I sniffed her surreptitiously, trying to switch on primeval senses, sure that she would smell different: farmyard, or chemical. I encountered only toothpaste and soap.

Perhaps the baby would be a girl; I wanted to be a Nice Auntie, the one she could talk to when her mother didn't understand. I could take her to galleries and the theatre and buy her books. But if I stayed in Scotland that wouldn't happen. I'd be unfamiliar, a name on the birthday cards, the sender of Christmas presents covered in postage stamps. There'd be family photographs with my face missing, like a black sheep. My niece would be taller each time I stepped off the train. And she would think of me as her Scottish auntie.

'What did Peter say?' I asked. My sister looked shifty.

'Well, I wasn't quite sure until today, so I sort of haven't told him yet. It was a bit of an accident that I told you.'

'Oh, we'll keep schtum!' said my mother, making as if to zip her mouth closed.

'Hah!' I said, 'You'd better hurry up and tell him, Meg, or she'll beat you to it!' We all laughed with feeling because we knew it was true. But, until she told him, we were sharing a secret again, if only for a short time. Possibly the last one. In the darkness, I hugged myself.

They woke us at three-thirty, kicking the door, throwing the lights on. The PoweR Cut's had ended while we slept.

''Ello 'ello, what's all this then? Three girls in a bed!'

My brother-in-law licked an imaginary pencil, wrote in an invisible notebook.

'We apprehended the three girls in one bed . . .'

We were sleepy, too hot, annoyed.

'Did you catch anything?'

'I caught a bramah!' said Peter. 'Salmon for tea tomorrow!' They had no qualms about waking us at that time of the morning. Peter laughed and joked, showing off, and I gave him a tooth-baring smile, as silent and sincere as a pike.

We shooshed them out of the room while we got dressed. My mother, always slow to wake, sat grizzling against the headboard where we had propped her, while my sister and I hunted for clothes in the folds of the bed. She whispered to me, 'I won't tell Peter yet, he's still excited about the fish. In the morning, right?'

What was important. What wasn't important. I figured she'd cope with a baby just fine. With another baby.

'Excited about the fish, indeed!'

'I know; it's just easier.' She looked into my face and, in the half-light, I saw her likeness to my mother. 'You'll come and see us when the baby's born, right?'

'Right!'

She'd known my decision before I had. We sat together in silence at the edge of the bed and swung our legs. Two girls up a tree.

Second Hand

'RHONA, I'M COLD. I want to get down.'

But Rhona grasps Melanie's goosey shoulders and holds her there. Body heat slides between them like a slip of paper. In the draught from the window, the waist-high net curtain dances a hula on their thighs.

'He hasn't seen us yet,' says Rhona firmly.

Melanie hears the house creeping up on them; doors whisper on their hinges, the staircarpet concertinas up on itself, ready to explode into the bedroom and catch them. But Rhona seems oblivious.

In the garden next door, Mr Lewis bends, slow as a branch, and digs his fingers into the earth. The udder of his brown trousers droops and swings between his legs. There is nothing to do in the garden in December; he has come to get away from Mrs Lewis.

'Turn around!' whispers Rhona as if he can hear her. Melanie wills him to stay there forever, to root his clodded boots in the soil and grow like a tree; but then he straightens and turns, almost as if they had called him, and looks up. Now they can leap, falling back from the window and tumbling on the carpet, giggling and ticklish.

'Excellent! Oh, excellent!' shrieks Rhona, kicking wildly. 'The timing was perfect! He'll never know if he saw us or not!' It is part of her plan to drive Mr Lewis mad.

'He'd better not. My mother would have my guts for garters.'

'He won't – he'll never be sure. We should have written "hello" on our chests! We should've written "hello" on mine and "Mr Lewis" on yours.' She looks at Melanie. 'See? It was good, wasn't it?'

Melanie shakes her head and smiles. She crawls over to the window, burning her knees on the gritty carpet, and peeps through the curtains.

'He's just standing and looking around. I know! Let's get dressed really quickly and run round by the lane, and stroll past like we're coming back from somewhere.'

'Yeah!'

But neither of them wants to move. The bedroom is cosy, and the house has changed its mind about ambushing them. It is enough for them to sit naked together and pretend it's normal. Melanie shuffles, reading the carpet's Braille with her bottom, and rubs a cool glass dolphin along her leg.

Rhona's house is a lawless place. You can touch anything, play with anything, stack things by size or by colour, or by how much you like them. The rooms migrate into each other, so there is a lawnmower in the bathroom and books in the beds and Rhona's father in the kitchen. But even Melanie has to admit that it's a mess. You can put a cup of tea down and not find it again for weeks. Each junk-shop armchair is different, and the cats are allowed to pick and scrabble at them as if there are diamonds hidden in the upholstery. In the dining room, a big picture of Jesus has leaned against the wall for two years, waiting to be nailed up.

Rhona herself wears Enid Blyton clothes: print dresses that skim her ankle socks, and a school blazer for a coat. In sewing class, the teacher is always happening to find lengths of spare cloth in the needlework cupboard, and she helps Rhona to make skirts and blouses; but when Melanie comes up with the teacloth that she has been stitching all term, Miss Downie just says: 'Unpick it and start again,' then, 'Well I never, Rhona! Here's a zip that might just fit . . .'

* * *

Melanie stages a fight between two Victorian dolls, and asks casually:

'Rhona – are you poor?'

Rhona looks up from drawing on her feet. 'No.' She draws a question mark on her big toe. 'Why?'

'Dunno. Just wondered.'

After a pause, Rhona says, 'My father's going to buy a car.'

'Yeah?'

'Yeah, he's going to teach me to drive it.'

'You can't drive, you're too young.' Melanie is angry with the lie. Rhona *said* she wasn't poor; she doesn't have to make things up to impress.

'You can drive on private land. My father knows a farmer who'll let us.'

'You can drive in Mr Lewis' garden, then. That'll definitely push him over the edge.'

Melanie referees while Victoria holds Felicity in a half-nelson for a count of one–two–three–break! The dolls get up and shake hands. 'I went on a tractor once,' she says, unconvincingly. Rhona rolls her eyes.

'That's living all right!'

Melanie looks at her wristwatch, the only thing she kept on.

'I have to go.'

She pulls on her jeans with the pants still inside and imagines being Rhona. Dressing here each morning among the seashells and kites and ex-Army sleeping bags. Having a mother who knocks gently on bedroom doors instead of screaming up the stairs about eggs being like bullets. Then she reaches under the bed for her trainers and finds a dust bunny the size of a netball, and one of the cats sucking her shoelace.

'I'm off,' she says.

'Thought I could smell something funny!' flashes back Rhona.

Running home, Melanie wonders if Rhona knows there's a smell to her house, and if her own house would smell as strange if she wasn't used to it.

'She's had that coat.'

Melanie's house smells of fish fingers and mint, and it sounds of television. Her mother is unwrapping After Eights and trying to remember how the posh girl eats them in the pre-Christmas adverts.

'That's the last you'll see of that!' she adds, nibbling daintily at the chocolate corners.

Melanie can't find her coat. Her mother won't let up about it, seems pleased to have something to moan about; something bad to associate with Rhona. Melanie's father sits motionless in his chair, in the belief that this will render him invisible.

'I'll get it tomorrow,' mumbles Melanie.

'Oho, you think you're going there tomorrow, do you?'

'I have to, to get my coat.'

'Don't be clever; your father can go and get it.' Melanie and her father shout 'No!' in unison. 'You should be staying in and concentrating on your school work. Rhona's mother doesn't want *you* hanging around all the time.'

Rhona's mother hardly ever knows they're there. If she wanders into the dining room to find them making a tent or putting on a play, she says, 'Oh! Hello girruls!' and looks at Rhona as if she knows her from somewhere but can't remember her name.

'She doesn't mind,' says Melanie.

'*I* mind! Why can't you play with someone nice like Jane Alexander? You two were friends before that bloody girl came along.'

'Jane Alexander is a snob!'

'Jane Alexander's father is a solicitor! And her mother is a Brown Owl!'

Melanie bites her lip to drive out the image of Mrs Alexander, feathered and bespectacled, tearing at a mouse.

'Don't you laugh, smarty pants! Why don't you join the Brownies?'

'You said I should concentrate on my school work.'

'Don't be clever. Brownies would go on your report.'

'Brownies is Hobbies and Interests,' says Melanie's father.

'Responsibility, John! Brownies is Responsibility.'

Melanie thinks of the vivisection laboratory that she and Rhona made out of cardboard boxes the week before. The cats wouldn't stay put, so they filled it with soft toys. Then they stormed the lab and liberated them, wearing handkerchief masks and shouting 'Freedom for animals!'

'I've got hobbies and interests,' she says.

'Well, God knows what they are! What'll you put on your report? Hanging out with hippies and low-lifes and . . .'

'Gyppos.'

'Tinkers, John! They're tinkers.'

The phone rings and Melanie runs to answer it, knowing it will be Rhona. She's in a call box.

'I'm in a call box!'

'You don't have to shout.'

'What? Look, I've only got one coin. I'll think of a shape in ten minutes, and you think hard and see if you can guess what it is! Okay?'

'Wait! Did I leave my coat with you?'

'Eh? Your coat? No, I haven't seen it. Now, think of that shape in ten minutes and write it down. We'll compare them tomorrow. Bye! There go the.'

Melanie drags herself back to the living room. 'Rhona.'

'As if you haven't just spent all day with her. What did she want?'

Melanie hesitates. She can't mention the telepathy experiment. 'Oh, just to say she hasn't got my coat.' But her mother pounces:

'Knew about that, did she? I told you, she's stolen it. Or else it's lost in that shady, shanty . . .'

'Shithouse.'

'Shed, John! It's a shed, that's what it is . . . Melanie, where are you sloping off to?'

'Shi – toilet.'

Melanie sits on the toilet with a notebook and pencil, and concentrates. Then she lets her mind run free, receptive, but still no shape comes, or none that seems more likely than any other. Eventually she draws the shape of a coat, adding a round hood so that, if Rhona thought of a circle, she can say that's it. For extra insurance, she adds triangular collars and square pockets.

* * *

'A shield?' says Melanie the next day. 'Who ever thinks of a shield? What chance did that give me?'

'Why, what did you draw?' says Rhona. Her face falls. 'Oh. Are you still missing your coat?'

'Yeah.'

Rhona folds the paper again and again, creasing the edges with her nails. 'You can only ever do it seven times, even if you start with a piece the size of Wales. Mel. Mel, I didn't take your coat. I'm your best friend, Mel.'

'Yeah.'

'Melly. Smelly Melly. Come on . . . hey, do you want to see a secret?'

'It's not them fairies again, is it?'

'No, it's not fairies!'

''Cause we waited an hour . . .'

'Shut up! I was a kid then!'

It had been five months ago, sitting by the river while Rhona sang softly to attract the wee folk, and the mud soaked Melanie's shorts right through to the knickers.

'I got a hell of a row for my shorts.'

'Look, d'you want to see it or not?'

'What is it?'

'My father's Christmas present.' Wheedling, 'It's in the attic.'

'All right then. But quickly; I'm only supposed to have come for my coat.'

Melanie's father had recently been into their attic for the Christmas decorations. His feet dangled through the hole as he swore and dropped the torch, and his slippers doodlebugged one by one on to the landing. Afterwards, he banged the hatch shut and double-locked it as if the first Mrs Rochester were up there.

Rhona's attic is so completely integrated into the house that it has a sweet little ladder of its own that clangs as they climb it. At the top, they are welcomed by a tailor's dummy in a shroud, with a television ariel sticking from its neck like a surprised head.

'That's it,' says Rhona.

'What – the dummy?'

'No, stupid! The dummy's *wearing* it. It's a suit.'

Melanie walks a wary circle round the suit, expecting mouse heads to pop from the pockets and cuffs. Close up, it has a cabbage smell.

'So. Rhona. This suit . . . is knitted. It's a knitted suit, Rhona!'

'My mother made it!' says Rhona proudly. 'It's natural dyes and everything – that's why it's green.'

'Rhona! I mean – your dad's got to weigh twenty-five stone! He's going to look like the Quatermass experiment!'

'Oh, r-really?' says Rhona, sounding like her mother. 'And what's your father getting?'

'Socks and soaps and slippers and a packet of Whiffs to smoke on Boxing Day. In the shed. Outside if fine.' Melanie's father always laughs when he says that, but she doesn't know why.

'Well, I think it's boring.'

'Well, I think it's normal!'

Melanie turns away and mooches among the trunks and boxes. 'Any more secrets up here?'

'Well, there's *my* presents,' says Rhona shyly.

'You know your Christmas presents?'

'Don't you?'

'Some of them. Stuff I asked for. But I'm getting surprises too; I'm getting a Haunted House and Slime.'

'Oh, right; *surprises*!'

'I looked in the wardrobe. Why, what are you getting?'

Rhona draws a circle in the dust with her toe. 'Don't tell.'

'What?'

'Don't *tell*!'

'All right, all right! What?'

'A bike.' Rhona tilts her chin. 'See? We're not poor.'

Melanie stares, then punches the air. 'Great! A bike! That's brilliant, we can go on our bikes together now!' She usually has to give Rhona a backie, and Rhona's skirts get caught in the chain and look like they've been chewed by an oily shark. 'So, where is it?'

Melanie casts around the attic for the spokey shapes and proportions that seem so familiar until you try to draw them;

she tried for weeks in anticipation of her own birthday bike. 'Is that it? Under the curtain?' She draws it back in a velvety, stagey ripple. 'Yes, it – oh, wow, Rhona! It's a Chopper!'

'I know.' Rhona starts hopping around, nervous. 'Leave it now, Mel.'

'But Rhona, a Chopper is mega! You'll be like Ruth Williams, she's got a Chopper. Well, she did. She had a new one, and it wasn't even for Christmas; my mother says they must have a money tree in the garden.'

'Yeah,' says Rhona miserably. 'Leave it, Mel.'

'And it's red too! Ruth's was yellow, but red's best – and look, here's a bell to go on it, but it'll have to go on the side, because with Choppers . . . Oh.' Melanie stops just as Rhona shouts:

'Mel! I said *leave it*!'

The bell clatters and pings on the wooden beams.

'Rhona . . .' says Melanie, very carefully, 'Rhona, this is Ruth's bike.'

Rhona stares at her. 'It is *not*!'

It becomes very quiet in the attic. Melanie gets a faint buzz in her ears, as if she can hear the dust settling around them. Squinting at the bike, she sees the light red spray where paint has spattered on the chrome.

'Someone's resprayed this bike! Rhona, you . . . you big fibber!'

Rhona's face sets from the chin up: the mouth, the cheeks, until her shining eyes are all that seem alive.

'I didn't say I was getting a *new* one!'

'*Fibber*! I bet you've got my coat too!'

Rhona recoils as if she has been punched.

'Well, if that's what you think, you can go home *now*!'

'I will, then!'

Melanie crosses to the top of the ladder. For a second, Rhona blocks her way:

'Melanie! The bell was for you. It was *your* present!'

Melanie shakes her head. She pushes past and shins down the ladder until she can look up at Rhona's pink legs, the scraped knees under her skirt. Suddenly the day before seems shameful and dangerous and very long ago.

'You can send my coat back when you find it,' she hisses, and Rhona screams and stamps at Melanie's finger; but Melanie is away, running down the stairs, passing Rhona's mother.

'Hello!' purrs Mrs Knox, 'Playing chase, are you?' She hugs the idea to her bosom like a bouquet and sings, 'Coming! Ready or not!'

Melanie decides that, when she gets home, she will tell them that Rhona's mother is cuckoo and that Rhona is a thief.

Melanie's brown beret is too tight and she knows that, when she takes it off, her hair will be set in two layers like a cottage loaf. She tugs at her yellow neckerchief. It's strange to be in the school hall on a Saturday, with the smell of hymn books and stewed dinners still lingering. Mrs Price's piano is shrouded in the corner, cannily turned to the wall so that no-one will try to sit on it.

Melanie's Brownie outfit, in contrast to her usual school uniform, feels like playing in an 'away' strip. She's not sure she likes it, the way it mutes her individuality; earlier, a woman she didn't even know stopped her and pulled her socks up. Other Brownies appear here and there in the unusual adult crowd. They are all eating, all the time: home-made fairy cakes and scones, gingerbread men with mutilated limbs. Melanie's mother didn't bake anything, but she will be coming down later with a bag of old clothes for the second-hand stall. In deference to Mrs Alexander, she has been washing and ironing them all week; the *really* old clothes, the shameful ones, have been relegated to work duty. Melanie's father has been wearing them, digging the flower beds over for spring like a scarecrow gardener.

Most of the Brownies are in chatty gaggles, but Melanie sells raffle tickets alone. She is shy of talking to the other girls' parents and she has sold only six. Two of those she bought herself, although she has no interest in winning the *Half a Lamb, Courtesy of Fate and Son, Family Butchers*, or in the *'Humpty' Family! Knitted by the Ladies of the Mothers' Union*. She has seen the Humpty Family; they look as if they have waddled out of a nightmare.

Her mother comes into the hall, embarrassingly smart in a camel coat and lipstick. She looks awkward, not sure of the etiquette of carrying a large bin bag. Melanie swerves through the crowd to get to her, tugs on her arm.

'Mam, will you buy some raffle tickets off me? I've only sold six.'

'In a minute. I said, *in a minute*, Melanie! Where's Mrs Alexander? Ah.' Click click of her heels on the waxed parquet.

Melanie hates her mother's social face, the cringe and twang in her voice when she talks to Mrs Alexander.

'Hell-oh, Barbara! Doesn't it all look lovely!'

Mrs Alexander, who spends so much of her time with little girls, speaks to everyone like a child.

'Well! Haven't you brought a big bag! Well done! Let's see what we've got . . .'

Melanie's mother tips the bag out, smiling proudly at the crispness of her ironing and the smell of the extra conditioner that she put in the wash. Melanie reaches out to stroke one of her own baby bonnets: the soft yellow wool, the silky ribbons. She's amazed to think that she was ever that small, that her mother could hold her whole self in her arms. She delves further among the bootees and cardigans and scarves and, underneath it all, she finds her old coat.

Melanie looks up, but her mother is smirking into Mrs Alexander's face, nodding at something she says. She looks down again, gripping the edge of the trestle table, and the clothes seem to rustle and crawl. It is, it really is her coat, the one that went missing; and the sudden host of ideas makes her feel sick. Her mother looks down at her at last.

'For goodness' sake, Melanie! What's wrong with you?' she says, and then: 'Ah.'

Driving home, it starts to rain. Melanie takes the raffle tickets, warm from her pocket, and folds them; not even seven times, only four. She rips them into confetti and pushes them into the plastic ashtray in the door of the car.

Swishing along the wet street, they pass Rhona pedalling grimly up the hill. She wears a coat like a big cape and it parachutes out behind her. The bike sways with the effort of her pumping legs. Melanie's mother would normally say something on seeing Rhona, and Melanie would normally say something in agreement. But Melanie is not speaking to her mother. She draws circles and squares and shields on the steamy window; then she wipes them off with her yellow neckerchief.

One to be Sociable

THE CAT SWALLOW-DIVES off the top of the cupboard and arrives on the table in a compressed crouch. With one mean lash of its tail, it scrambles the neat piles of screws and nails and sends them boiling over the kitchen floor; then it is gone, and all he can do is strike at the quivering air where it was.

'You bugger!' he shouts. 'Excuse my French – no, come back here and *don't* excuse my French! You – you *miscreant*!'

He stops, astonished at the bark of his own voice in the lean-to kitchen, the echoed 't' tutting him. Deliberately, he thinks the same sentence again, tucking it back neatly into his head where it belongs. He catches himself picking at his hearing aid like a scab, and drops his hands. The hearing aid is never on – it runs down the batteries – but he got into the habit of wearing it to please his grandchildren. They used to call him the Bionic Man.

His diary is on the windowsill. He takes it down, opens it to the back and writes 'Strangulation', an addition to the list of ways in which he plans to kill the cat. He knows to spell it with a 'u', his spelling is impeccable (two 'c's'). He closes the diary and puts it back where he can see it. Its cover is so vividly turquoise that it makes him *feel* turquoise: cheerful and reassured.

Stooping, he claws at the screws, but they roll like mercury on the linoleum, and he decides that, after all, he can tidy the kitchen drawer tomorrow. It will be a job that he can start after dinner, something that will see him through to teatime.

* * *

He has learnt to stretch tasks. His son got him the diary from work, and he writes in it each morning:

Oil Clocks.

Then he oils the clocks. Then he puts a tick in his diary and writes:

Oiled Clocks.

He writes in his diary every day, with the thought that someone will read it in the future and know that he was never idle.

He loves the luxury of all that paper. At first he was afraid of it. The pages thin and Bible-whispering, rippled with their own compression. The gold-tinted edges that rubbed their sheen on his fingers. He would open it, feel its clean glare in his eyelids, and close it again. Then one day it came upon him to write the alphabet as he had learnt it in school, upper and lower case, keeping carefully to the thin blue tram lines. He wrote as if someone were watching him; did the alphabet twice, then wrote his full name, *Mr* and *Esq.*, and his address in the section at the front. He crossed out 'Blood Group', half-closing his eyes at the squeamish words, and after 'Car Registration' he wrote 'JAG 1' for a joke.

His own beautiful hand delighted him – they really taught you how to write in those days. He found he could recall the alphabet frieze on the school-house wall – an Apple, a Ball, a Cat, all the way to a Zebra, which he has never seen. He would rather have a zebra than the cat. He could keep it in the garden. He could write in his diary:

Feed Zebra.

And when it was munching hay in the shed:

Fed Zebra.

He could play his Xylophone to it and take it in his Yacht.

He can hear the cat breaking something upstairs, but can't be bothered to go up and stop it. It's like a bluebottle in any case, just circles back, intent on doing what it wants. He had accepted the cat at first. It was Cissie's pet, purring on her lap like an instrument that only she could play, or running ahead of her like a dodgem car, its tail up. It was company for her when he went down the Whit. Then he hated the cat for its selfish mourning, the way it followed the ghost of Cissie's routine around the house.

These days their life is a series of battles and truces. It saves him, at least, from the pain of trying to set mousetraps, and, when he touches Cissie's old armchair and finds it warm, he can tell himself that the cat was there not long before.

He tucks the diary under his arm and closes the door on the chaotic kitchen. In the living room, he puts the television on and, while it warms up, he checks the clocks. The wallpaper is shiny underneath them where his daughter-in-law wiped the oil off, scolding him.

'They run on batteries, Ted; you don't need to oil them!'

'Aye, but there's still the mechanism to consider.' Women know nothing.

'No there's not. They're Made in Taiwan.'

She always has plenty to say for herself. She and his daughter apportion him out – his shopping, his washing – so he has to bite his tongue. They go on Ted Duty, wriggling with righteousness, slotting him in between their office jobs and their own growing families. On their rare rendezvous, they discuss him over his head.

'I bought him a loaf, and he's got plenty of tins in.'

'You should have seen his sheets! I had to wash them twice.'

They extract embarrassment from him as a payment. Neither of them wants him for Christmas, and he doesn't want to go. It's only August and they're already arguing about it.

'I might be six feet under by then.' He fingers the euphemism like a dirty collar.

'Don't be silly, Ted! There's years in you yet.'

'Aye, Dad. You'll see us all out!'

And their eyes gleam.

He has written what he thinks of them in his diary, on the day of each of their birthdays. He knows they will look there first.

The programme warms into vision. It is one that Cissie used to watch, flipping her head back so that the screen reflected in her bifocals. It gave him a turn that, her eyes suddenly magnified to twice their size: four peepers, two large, two small. Staring at the spangly singers and cocky comedians like they were her own babies crawling around in the set. Like, if she blinked, they would disappear.

'It mesmerises you, that telly.'

'Hush, Ted!'

So he would take down his mothy coat, the hanging, grey chrysalis of himself, and flap into its soundless arms. He kept his eyes on the back of Cissie's curlered head while his hands, like feelers, secreted away his Mint Imperials, money, handkerchief. Then he would cough and hem, aiming for nonchalance as the thought, the idea of the pub fluttered in the dark draught of the door.

'Just off for a constitutional, love.'

'Don't come back drunk at all hours!'

'Physically impossible.'

'Eh?'

'Just one to be sociable!'

Important not to draw her attention from the television. One of those comedians, he knows for sure, goes bingeing on champagne and fights with policemen and smashes up his Rolls Royce practically every week. It's always in the papers.

'I'm locking the door at half past ten!'

'Just a few glasses –', closing the door, '– of sparkling champagne, m'dear!'

He's never tasted champagne. Champagne and a zebra; *please, Jim, could you fix it for me.* And Cissie back. He wants Cissie back to stop him going down the pub so that he wants to go. He hasn't wanted to go to the pub in ages.

The smell of her perfume is strong in the room. It goes beyond memory, makes him lift his head and sniff like a dog, scenting the wind. It's not in the cushions – he plumps them to his face to be sure – or in the antimacassars hanging like ragged sails on the becalmed sofa. He struggles to his feet and touches a hand to his heart, tries to analyse the emotion and finds he is . . . he's a little. Afraid.

The smell is stronger at the foot of the stairs. He turns off the television and takes a poker from the fireplace. The banister creaks to his slow weight, and the smell thickens as he ascends, makes him giddy. At the top of the stairs, he puts the poker down, feeling foolish. It's his own bedroom there, the same door that he must have painted ten times or more. Just the sight of a brushstroke can take him back years; crouching easily with a paint brush, dipping it in his tea by mistake. A gloss headache. He opens the door on to the scent, so strong now that it fills his eyes and mouth, and a movement on the dresser startles him: the cat, rubbing its face in a pool of perfume and broken glass. He roars and leaps at it, it's cornered against the mirrors, he sees its fighting reflection from three different angles, and his own six hands grasping the wet fur, then losing it, and it spits at him, and is gone.

He doesn't know what to do about the perfume. Spills are tricky, big for their size as problems go. After a while, he draws the curtain across and swirls it in the yellow liquid. The perfume was one thing that he'd kept. Cissie always used to recite: 'Perfume, like love, you must not hoard,' but he'd kept this like a drug, sniffing at the bottle cap whenever he woke in the night. Now it will evaporate and fade, go stale. His daughter-in-law will pull down the curtain with her wash-day hands and scold him again. He opens the wardrobe and wipes his own hands in the scarves and waistcoats, in the hats that they won't be able to wash. He picks out one of the hats and perches it on his head. Then he takes out his summer coat, the brown one, and puts it on, closing the wardrobe door gently to preserve the scent. In the mirror he tells his three selves:

'Just one to be sociable.'

If there were five mirrors, he would look like Five Boys chocolate. He runs his face through the expressions: *Desperation*, *Expectation*. What are the others? He can't remember. He closes his eyes to recall the taste, the thick melt. The fifth one – that's it, for definite – *Realisation*! His skin prickles and flushes at the unaccustomed effort.

* * *

He has been coming to the Whit since he was a boy, since he used to watch the Hunt meet, holding bridles for money. He met Cissie here at one of the Bingo nights that seemed to bring the women swarming like gnats. You heard them buzzing in the lounge next door, the occasional loud shriek of laughter; then a gang of you just happened to meet them outside, picking out your chosen one. Letting Ernie have flighty Mary, who would end up running off with a farmer.

This is the first time in his life that he has been here alone. Now, instead of horses, there is horse power; red cars parked at challenging angles. And new, outsized umbrellas, and shrubs in tubs. People have used the tubs as bins, filled them with crisp bags. The inn sign has been changed to a stylised picture of Dick Whittington's cat, which is a woman which is dressed as a cat, with a come-hither look that makes him shiver. The Whit itself has been painted pink, draped with coloured lights, unexpected and nauseating as a bad pint. He feels he could reach out and push this facade. It would teeter back, sway forward again, falling, landing in the car park with a boom and a shudder, and he could step over the boards and into his own, real pub. But the car park is full of Dangerous Youths.

He often imagines Dangerous Youths breaking into his house so that he can fell them with his boxing skills and get his name in the papers. *Feisty Pensioner, Ted Robertson* . . . He even keeps a hammer handy in case his boxing skills desert him. *Police praised the heroic grandfather for his presence of mind* . . . When he sees them in the streets in twos and threes, his heart thrums like a ship's engine at the thought of having a go. But there are too many of them. They probably have a list of their own: How to Kill Old Men Who Want to Get into the Pub.

He scratches his hearing aid, runs his tongue around his teeth. To go back now would be a worse defeat than going in. Reaching into his coat, he turns his hearing aid on. *Senior Citizen in Brave Pub Decision . . .*

The youths jeer him, cheer him on:

'Left–right–left–right!'

'Oi! Oi, Granddad!'

Singing: 'Granddad, Granddad, we love you . . .'

The only courtesy comes from a fat boy, strangely smart in a dinner jacket, who holds the door open for him.

An impostor staircase catches him by surprise and topples him like Chaplin into a plastic tree that catches him in a saucy embrace. He apologises to it and sets out over the fun-house floor, swaying a wavering line through the crowd, the carpet-boards-carpet tricking him like a maze. A frieze of televisions runs around the wall; sport and music and more channels than he knew existed, more noise than he could have imagined. The only thing he recognises is his own sad reflection in the mirrored far wall, a crouching, ghostly tortoise in a coat like a brown paper bag. He watches his own mouth working, fishy and frightened. This is not his place anymore. One drink, to say he did it, and then he will go.

But he can't get served, though he dips his sleeves in the puddled bar, taps a coin, puffs himself like a bullfrog to claim space, attention. The barmaid has a pierced eyebrow; she glides towards a new arrival, a young man with a nose ring, like they were magnetised.

He takes up a menu as barmaid-bait. It tells him that the pies are *delicious*!, that the onion rings are *tasty*!, and that he could have something that looks like *tarantula*! if he could get someone's attention. It warns him of *Death by Choclate*! and he takes out his pen and carefully forms the missing second 'o', one circle to make the shape, another on top to thicken it. The barmaid throws her arms in the air and waves them – a new dance, or religious ecstasy, he can't decide. Perhaps she's had a shock from the new electric pumps. Her mouth moves silently, and he turns his hearing aid up, and then the fat boy is beside him.

'I'm glad you're here,' he says.

'You're out.'

'Eh?'

'Come on – out you go. Bloody old vandal, you are.'

'No, hang about . . .'

Again in the mirror he sees himself grapple and waltz with the boy in the suit, back towards the door, and now he has everyone's attention. The men nudge the women as if it's their joke, as if they set it up, and the room runs past him, a Girl, a Table, a Door, *pensioner murdered in pub brawl*, and, oh God, one of the youths is coming over to join in; he grasps Ted by the shoulders and yells:

'Oi! Steady on, Granddad!'

He bleats and flails, but he can't get a decent swing, and the boy pins his arms and shouts again:

'Granddad! It's me! Craig!'

Ted drops his arms. 'Craig?' He looks into the boy's face. It's his own grandson; he never recognised him. 'Craig!' he says again, 'Craig, you're . . . you're a Dangerous Youth!'

'Is he with you?' asks Fat Boy.

'Aye,' says Craig.

'Well, he was defacing a menu.'

'I was rectifying an error!'

'Ah, leave him be, Billy,' says Craig, and mouths the word 'old'.

Fat Boy drops his shoulders. 'Well, look after him then.'

'Right you are,' says Craig. 'C'mon, Granddad. I'm getting a team for the pub quiz.'

'Pub quiz, is it? General knowledge and that?'

'Aye. C'mon, what you drinking?'

'Oh. Ah. There's a revelation! I didn't know you were eighteen yet.'

'Near enough. C'mon, Granddad, sit down.'

'Canberra!'

'Hush, Granddad! You're just supposed to press the button, right? A, B or C.'

'Is he sure about that?' Craig's friends crowd in, an anxious scrum. 'I thought it was Sydney.'

'Canberra,' he whispers. 'For *definite*.'

'Press B, then.'

'If he's wrong . . .'

He presses B on the console and they turn to the screen on the wall, waiting, then:

'Yes!'

'Result!'

'I told you – Canberra!' He holds his arms aloft in a 'champion' attitude: 'Good on yer, sport!' The boys laugh.

He is starting to tell them apart now. None of them has much hair; they're all tattooed and shaved like an army louse clinic, but they let him run his hand over their suede heads, and offer to get him a haircut the same.

'It wouldn't take long,' he says. 'I'm not very hirsute.'

'I bet you *are* hirsute; we just need to find you the right girl,' says the one called Andrew, and the others shout:

'Oh *An*-drew!'

One of the boys passes him a roll up, and he takes a little, giddying puff, lets out the smoke in a whinny.

'What's this – Turkish snout, is it?'

'Aye, that's right. Turkish!'

'Turkish Delight,' he says, and Craig folds into convulsed laughter. They seem to have clicked with their sense of humour; something in the genes no doubt. And the boy's looking after him, they all are. He hasn't had to buy a drink all night.

'No, no,' they say, 'you're the team mascot!'

'Mascot, be damned! I'm the brains of this outfit!'

They start singing the *Mastermind* theme, and someone shouts:

'Keep it down, boys!'

'Boys!' he says, pretending to be affronted. He takes a swallow of beer and squints at the screen for the next question. 'Louis the Fourteenth!' he yells, 'For *definite*!'

It's dark now. They sway out of the pub together and stand in a huddle, giggling. Suddenly, Craig's friends remind him of the Five Boys slogan, and he points at each of them in turn:

'*Desperation - Pacification - Expectation - Acclamation - Realisation*!'

There is a pause. 'Craig,' says one of the boys, 'I think we've fried your Granddad's brain.'

'I'd better give him a lift,' says Craig. 'Hey, Granddad, ever had a backie before?'

'A backie?'

'On a motorbike.'

'A *motor*bike!' He doesn't know how he will fit all this in his diary. He'll have to write really small.

Two of the boys slot him on to the seat of the bike like a clothes peg. He has a brief, remembered moment of gas-mask panic at the passenger's helmet, then relaxes and starts to preen in it.

'Three rules,' says Craig. 'Rule one – hold on tight. Rule two – hold on tight! And rule three –' he kicks the engine into life and they yell together:

'Hold–On–*Tight*!'

The journey takes no time and forever, and he knows he will remember it like an accident, though they arrive smoothly and safely. The neighbours' curtains don't even twitch. The cat comes to the door, wanting to prowl outside, but bolts back into the house when it sees him bent double on the path, and Craig grappling with his alien head. The helmet plops off and he rubs his ears. A wedge of plastic comes away in his hand.

'Craig, look!' he says, 'the Bionic Man!'

'Aye, that's right!'

But he's not sure that the boy remembers.

'Uh, d'you want to come in for a spot of tea or something?'

'No thanks, better be going. Next time, eh?'

'Aye. Next time!'

He closes the door, and the windows rattle to the sound of the bike taking off.

He feeds the cat in the dark, too dark to note it in his diary, but he will put it in tomorrow. He will fill in all the day's events then, and when he has done that, he will tidy the kitchen drawer. Then he'll oil the clocks. Or he might leave them a day. Anything could happen!

Still in the dark, he sits in the armchair for a moment, gathering his strength for the climb upstairs; but his eyes drift closed.

The cat creeps forward out of its corner and sniffs at his boots.

He doesn't move as it climbs carefully up his leg and stands balanced on his lap, looking into his face. Slowly, it stretches out and licks his cheek, just once, and he stirs, smiling.

'Goodnight, Cissie,' he says.

Fantastic

ALL THEIR FAMILY outings began like this. She stared at the shoulders of her mother's floral dress, willing it to spontaneously combust and set her new perm alight. The tar-stink of perming fluid filled the Land Rover, mingling with shaving foam, toothpaste, perfume; but she knew they would all smell of sheep when they got out.

'Barbecue,' she said. '*Bar–B–Q.*'

'Shut up, Gillian.' Her mother didn't turn around, but her brother did, wagging his tongue over the back of the seat. She longed for a pair of shears.

'Not a garden party! We'll be the only ones wearing frocks!'

'Shut up! Don't you *dare* show me up tonight!'

Her mother feared showing up the way other people feared death. Gillian tilted her chin; she had already formed a plan to be dignified and aloof, to waft in the background with a secret smile, gliding in and out of the conversations like a swan. She would be enigmatic, which sounded like something mechanical but meant cool. But before she could stop herself, she thought *New Persil Enigmatic – gets your clothes mysteriously clean*, and the word was spoilt.

'Anyway, that pinafore's very Laura Ashley.' Her mother said it as one word, verylauraashley, which really meant: Not Laura Ashley. Cheap imitation. Everyone would know. And her sister had copied her outfit, as if they were still little girls whose mother dressed them alike.

'I'm not playing with the kids either!'

'*Don't show me up*! And take that . . . that *moue* off your face!'

'Moo! Moo!' said her brother, and her father laughed.

'Moo-cows, eh?' His face was florid with sunburn, except for the white line on his forehead where his flat hat had been. He looked raw and sheared. 'Help Daddy with the moo-cows!'

He turned off the engine and the Land Rover spasmed to a stop, wide tyres foaming on the gravel drive. From their high seats they could look down into Uncle Keith's Jaguar, see the expensive detritus that Aunty Sylvia had left in the passenger's footwell. A gold lipstick, a crumpled silk scarf; she yearned for them, suddenly and completely.

'Showing off,' commented her mother, struggling to unhook her skirt from the gear stick; showing off was worse than showing up. Gillian got out of the Land Rover with careful decorum. Her brother and sister tumbled out of the back, yelping and racing, and her mother caught them by their collars and boomeranged them back, yanking their clothes straight, spanking them clean. They didn't suit their best outfits. They looked like a Louis Wain illustration: cats and dogs on a Sunday School outing. She fought with the bodice of the dress, willing it to be looser, but there were already two circles of sweat under her arms.

'Fantastic! You're here!'

Aunty Sylvia. Turquoise toenails, a snake of gold bracelets up her arm. A T-shirt reading 'Flaunt it!' over skinny brown legs. Next to her, Gillian's mother looked like a Beatrix Potter hedgehog, as if the perm went right down her back and was waiting to prickle through the cloth. Even her voice seemed to weigh more; you could only tell they were sisters by their jealousy. Gillian fell into her aunt's perfumed hug, peering over her shoulder to the garden. One woman, in fat white leggings and a 'Frankie Says' T-shirt, looked like a pulled tooth, but the rest of the guests might have fallen off Ralph Lauren's yacht. No-one else was upholstered in a verylauraashley frock.

Sylvia kissed Gillian's mother.

'Fantastic shoes, Viv! But d'you want to borrow a pair of

flatties for the lawn? Mine would be too small, but Keith's got some espadrilles . . .'

'I'm quite comfy, Sylvia; don't fuss!'

Her mother hobbled on to the patio, leaving spidery clods of mud with heel-holes in them. She poised herself over a lounger, and its legs gave a final little death-kick then were still as she dropped herself into it. Gillian watched Aunty Sylvia go to work on her father: pinching his shoulder, petting his biceps, and where *did* he get that *fantastic* tan?

'Out in the fields.' It was Sylvia's tease that her father was a gruff-but-seductive son of the soil, and he played up to it. 'Handling the livestock!'

Gillian thought it sounded filthy. Aunty Sylvia squealed:

'You *hunk*!'

'Oh, Sylv,' her mother moved to intervene, 'I brought lamb chops, but they haven't been out of the freezer long . . .'

'Keith'll nuke them in the micro . . . Keith . . . !'

'I'll take them!' Gillian wanted to score points; none of the kids would have offered, and she could sit in the kitchen and pretend that Uncle Keith was her father.

Uncle Keith was mixing drinks, wearing an apron with a barmaid's torso on it for a joke. Her own family would never have bought clothes for a joke.

'Hiya, kid!' He called everyone 'kid', so that was all right. 'Killer Martinis! Try that,' pouring a half-glass from the pitcher. 'Is it dry enough?' She didn't know what he meant, took a sip anyway, felt lemon tears prickle in her eyes.

'Yes!' she squeaked. He topped the glass up.

'Don't tell Vivienne. Our secret, right?'

Vivienne! Not 'your mother', or, worse, 'Mammy'. She sat on a corner stool, tried several poses for maximum glamour, held the drink like an accessory. She remembered the chops and dumped them on the table.

'Lamb chops, Uncle Keith! Still a bit frozen.'

'Thanks, kid!'

He spilled them on to a plate, slid the plate into the microwave and pressed a button with his elbow, waving his hands to show her:

'Hygiene!'

She watched him move around the kitchen like a TV chef, shaking the pans to make them hiss and steam, protecting his hands with a folded navy dishcloth. Her mother had two oven mitts in the shape of a Dutch boy and a Dutch girl with cauterised faces. *Double Dutch: putting the 'kitsch' into 'kitchen'.*

Uncle Keith chopped a sheaf of herbs on a wooden board, the knife performing a rapid cha-cha-cha across the fresh, dark green. She loved to watch him cook. He didn't need to be able to; he had his own business, he was already useful enough. But he liked to do it. Her father, by contrast, seemed made for the fields; when he came indoors, he blinked at the change of light, and blundered against the furniture like a cat in a dolls' house. He wouldn't have known coriander from cannabis, but Uncle Keith did. He was *sophisticated.* He'd been the first person in town to own a red striped shirt, and now everyone had them. She smelt his aftershave as he reached over her head to the cupboard.

'Nice dress,' he said.

'Ugh, no!' She blushed. 'It makes me look like a country bumpkin!'

'No way! You look like – like Tess of the d'Urbervilles!'

Aunty Sylvia rushed into the kitchen, skidding in her strappy sandals.

'Bloody Italian tiles,' she said, in case anyone was around who ought to know, then, 'Keith, there you are!' Her face was flushed, the social mask seeming to slide off with her sweat. 'The barbecue's doing something funny!'

'Okay, kid!' Keith never got flustered. He wiped his hands and went to tend to it, patting Sylvia's bottom on the way past.

Sylvia looked at her.

'Are you cold, Gillian? D'you want to borrow a cardigan?'

'No. Yes!'

Sylvia loved to lend out clothes in a proprietorial way, making her guests belong to her. Gillian's mother said she did it so you'd see the labels. That was why Gillian liked it; it was a rare chance to wear Jaeger and Yves Saint Laurent, to imagine yourself rich. 'Yes, please,' she said. But Sylvia brought her a baggy gardening sweater. Marks and Spencer. It reached her knees.

'The kids are out by the trees,' said Sylvia. 'Would you keep an eye on them? Fantastic!'

Sylvia dumping her with the children; she wasn't going to fall for *that*! It was too easy to get involved in some stupid game, and the next thing you knew you were counting to a hundred or climbing trees; you were *playing*. She hadn't spent an hour putting make-up on to *play*. When Sylvia wasn't looking, she peeled off like a Spitfire leaving its squadron and circled back to the patio. She picked an old deckchair that no-one would want to take off her and set it up in a quiet corner, where she could see everything going on, could hear people talking and imagine herself making smart remarks in reply. It was like being a ghost. The conversation drifted through the barbecue smoke, strident, then soft again . . . *fantastic* holiday, we lived just like the natives . . . of course he's gay, have you seen his house? . . . well that's her third appendectomy, if you know what I mean . . . She heard her father's voice, heavily patient: '. . . but sheep *are* free range . . .', and a man vowing loudly to sack his accountant.

Her mother sat alone, too close to the *BugBusta* torch, and slapped her arms.

'I'm a bloody magnet for these things!' she muttered, then, 'Jesus, Gillian! Do you have to sit on my shoulder like a gargoyle? Bloody eavesdropping!'

'Listening!'

'*Eavesdropping*!'

'How can I be eavesdropping? No-one's talking to *you*!'

Her mother's mouth pursed up tight, lips disappearing like a scarf tucked into a magician's hand.

'You shouldn't smile so much, Gillian; everyone can see your fillings!'

Gillian gasped and leaned back into the shadows. 'You cow!' she whispered. 'You bloody old cow!'

* * *

A black jeep squealed up the drive like a girl, skipped to a stop. It's horn played an American fanfare, short and loud, and a skinny man jumped out. He wore a silk shirt and leather jeans, outsized sunglasses, and his face was as brown and wrinkled as the bark of a tree.

'Your git's arrived,' observed her father.

'Toby! Fantastic!'

'Sylvia, sweetheart!'

They kissed, mwa mwa, and Sylvia grasped the skinny man around the waist.

'You remember Toby, don't you? He's a musician.'

'In music *production*,' corrected Toby. He spoke like a Radio One DJ. 'Sylv's sister, am I right? Hi! And hubby's here too!' He put out his hand, but her father pretended not to see it.

'You shouldn't park your van behind the Land Rover,' he said. 'I might forget it's there and back over it.'

'Right! Crazy guy!' Toby laughed. He spotted Keith coming out to the barbecue. 'Keith! You old bastard! The Keithster! The Keith Man!'

'Hiya kid!' They hugged each other, making her father hiss through his teeth. 'How's London?'

'Lady London is a *bitch* – she's breaking my heart! Pour me a drink, you old sod . . .'

'Ponce,' said her father. Her mother snorted.

'Just because he dresses nice! It wouldn't hurt you once in a while . . .'

But her father's face was closed, not listening. His hand crept to his arm, touching his own reassuring muscle, and she realised that he was *jealous*: not of Toby and her mother, but of Toby and *Sylvia*. She took in a little whoosh of breath; it was the first piece of adult information that she'd worked out on her own, without eavesdropping, or having to have it explained like she was the last to know. No wonder her mother didn't like Sylvia.

Dusk was deepening into night. She crept to the punch bowl, poured herself a glass: spicy red liquid, plopping chunks of fruit. The barbecue glowed in the evening breeze, and she slipped off her sweater, letting the warm-cool air raise the tiny, hackling hairs on her arms. On the patio, her father was sulking, frowning at a cocktail umbrella that someone had stuck in his beer. Everyone else was talking and laughing, doing it just right, like extras in a television play about a party. A nice party, too, with things to eat that you didn't recognise, things that burnt your mouth, or that would make you smell the next day. Toby was talking about 'the biz', and she smiled at him, then remembered and closed her mouth. She forced herself to eat an olive, had to wash the taste away with a gulp of punch, but she tipped her head back too far and got a faceful of sliced orange, red dregs and sludge down her chest.

'Oh shit!'

Toby tittered.

'Gillian!' her mother kicked to get out of the lounger, her father frowned at her as if he didn't know who she was. Her brother galloped by on an invisible horsie.

'Sick!' he shouted, pointing at her. Her mother rolled her eyes dramatically and said:

'I'm sorry about Gillian, everybody. She's going through an "ugly duckling" phase!'

She turned and ran.

'Hiya, kid! Enjoying yourself? Oho, what happened to you?'

'It's not sick!'

'No way!' Keith handed her a dishcloth and watched as she mopped herself down. 'Better?'

'Fantastic!' she said miserably.

'Poor baby! Tell you what,' he said, 'we're out of glasses. There's a dozen more in the larder – you know where the larder is?'

She nodded vigorously. 'Back of the house, down the stairs.'

'Good. So, take this tray. The glasses are on the top shelf, next to the jam. Got that?'

'Top of the shelf, next to jam.'

Keith laughed.

'Not too tipsy, are you?'

'No way!'

'Be careful, then.'

She found the jam straight away, but she couldn't find any glasses. She put the tray down and dragged a wine crate across the floor, stood on it and felt to the back of the shelf. Thick dust, a dead spider cringed in on itself, but no glasses. Perhaps he'd meant another shelf. She sighed; she didn't want to go back without them. There was nothing worse than someone having to come and say: look, there they were all along.

The larder was huge, not a cupboard but a room; the lawn-mower was in there, and a coat rack full of Barbours and Burberrys. Underneath was a row of riding boots, pale mud dried on the toes. She listened against the door for a moment, then kicked off her sandals and tried on the biggest pair of boots, but they flopped around. The next pair were snug, hugged her bare calves. She was thrilled by the thought that they were probably Aunty Sylvia's. Suddenly, although she hadn't heard footsteps, the larder door opened; she managed to pull off one of the boots, but then Uncle Keith was in the room with her.

'No luck?' He saw the boot, still on her leg, and smiled. 'Well, look at Cinderella!'

'I'm sorry! I was only trying it!'

'No probs, kid, no probs!'

He closed the door behind him.

'Here, let's help you off with that.' He kneeled down. 'Your foot, milady!'

Laughing, she placed her heel in his outstretched hands. He tugged, grunted, no good; grasped her ankle, tried again, moved his hands to the top of the boot, wriggling it. She felt his thumbs pressing her skin through the leather. His fingers, clean nails, the top of his head, hairs dark and defined in a whorl on his scalp, and the barbecue smell, burnt lamb fat, gin on his breath as he looked up at her.

His hand on her thigh was happening, real and heavy. And all she could think of was a dog that wanted to shake paws.

She placed her hand on his.

Her voice was clear and firm.

'Down, boy!'

'Eh?'

'Ba–ad dog!' She wagged her finger, turning it into a joke. He looked confused, sat back on his haunches, fat and ridiculous.

The boot came off easily then. She passed it to him like a problem and glided out, over the Italian tiles, feeling the rough patio stones, and the cool grass on her feet. Halfway across the lawn, she stopped. Under the trees, the children chattered and hooted, sleepy night birds. Near the house, the adults bleated and bayed, greedy and territorial. Flashes in the darkness like teeth and claws. She arched her neck and hissed.

From the Life

I SAT IN THE DARK for nearly an hour, looking at the little figures on the ice. Were they skating? Some had their arms out, like the thin, black bird that flew in the foreground. Most seemed to be there for the hell of it, the thrill of walking where you couldn't trust your steps. As a child I'd loved this picture because the hunters in the snow looked like my dad when he walked the dogs. The painted umber hounds, the plump, darting terriers – I had named them all, and recalled them now like friends in a school photograph.

The Fine Art Museum was empty, the silence so acute that it hissed. I'd spent a while in the Egyptian Rooms. They were bright with primrose light, but there was a coldness too: death-cult of mummification. I had felt panic like a cobweb in my mouth, imagined too easily the lips rustling with papyrus words, the leaf-lidded autumn eyes opening to see me. But the Brueghel Room was as dark and as safe as a wood. I sat on the hard, black bench and thought myself into the painting.

I invoked Pieter Brueghel. I gave him a big hat and a pencil, watched him blow grey, warming puffs into his hands. He stood on the hillside with snow to his ankles, listening to the screams of the skaters, sketching them, then went home and tried to remember the scene. He would write *naer het leven* on the back of his studies: from the life.

'Thank you!' I whispered. A curator, creaking past in a blue uniform, frowned and peered. I was grateful for the cool of the scene. The grassy ice, the colour of the Danube; not blue at all. Even the fire to the left of the picture was bitter-chill, a fire with frost in it. I remembered a quote, 'he had painted the unpaintable, the actual feel of winter cold'. That would be my strongest memory of Vienna, I thought: the cool, dark room in the heat of summer.

Back at the hotel, I came out of the shower to find Iain picking through his e-mail. The tick and chuckle of the lap-top was familiar, the only thing left of home. Even my sweat smelt different, like the dusty hotel milk: UHT perspiration. The Canadian Me had been sweated out, and Europe was in my bones and tissues, ingested with the food and the air.

> Welcome in Vienna.

'It's from Danielle!' I sat up on the bed. 'What does she say?'

> I hope your hotel is good and there is plenty of nice food and BEER Iain, ha ha. I see you are a hundred degrees there, phew! Dave says Hi and Stéphane too, but he is stupid. Work is too boring, except for Levin. He sends another e-mail to everyone and it becomes nasty. We have Dunkin Donuts yesterday and the students eat all the good one. I'm going to bed now, what time is it with you? Bye, guys.

'It must have been late when she sent that . . .' I said.

'. . . from the way her English slips, yeah. It's cute.'

'Shall I send her one back?'

'Be quick, then. And put something on, don't sweat all over the keyboard.'

I sat on the edge of the bed with a towel on my knees; detergent-hardened terylene with 'Hotel Aramis' picked out in tan, reversed on the other side. Iain passed me the computer as if it were a baby.

> Danielle! Thanx for the message, chickie. It's too damn hot here, I'm melting! The food is okay but meaty. We found a nice

> pizza place last night, but after we'd finished eating, a cockroach came out and did a cabaret on the table. Who is Levin? Why is he sending nasty messages? Send more e-mail, I need some English, even yours, ha ha. Kiss Montreal for me. Or not, as you wish.

The actual feel of winter cold. A mountain of city windows, and snow to our ankles. Meeting

'Danielle Tremblay! Hi! You're the new professor, right? Welcome to Mitchell!'

The first and last time we will feel her vigorous handshake; from then on it is always the 'bec', the left–right–left Québecois kiss.

'I'll take you to your office! Come, follow me.'

At the centre of the building there are no windows, just yellow light and the taste of air-conditioning. You wouldn't know it was December.

'Is that all your coat? Boy, you'll freeze! See these corridors, they are from the student riots in the sixties. They changed the block so we can only riot in pairs now. See here,' opening a door, 'the Computer Labo.' A few students look up and mutter Hi. 'I live in that room!'

We have to jog to keep up with her. There are conference posters on the corridor walls, calls for papers, cartoons about computers clipped from magazines. The biggest pin-up is Einstein. The names on the doors are people who will become our friends: Dave Grossman, Stéphane Martin. We will stop hearing their accents, and our own accents will become muted, the tonal peaks and valleys flattening into negotiable terrain for North Americans. Treacherously, we will give up correcting people who say we're English.

The Oriental students have colonised one end of the corridor and Danielle reads their names aloud, giggling, exaggerating them to sound like the ricochet of bullets.

'Tang! Chong! Tao! It's like a shoot-out here!' She taps at her own door, 'Chez moi!' Knock knock. 'But I'm not in!' Then she stops suddenly and frowns. 'Hey, do you guys have plans to eat tonight? Because . . .'

The catch-in-the-throat kindness. And someone has already put Iain's name plate on his office door, the pen line fattening with hesitation on the second 'i'.

'Look!' Danielle bashes the door open. 'You have a window! You see it all from here!'

Montreal in the snow.

I woke with a burning pain in my stomach, a familiar ache.

'I think I've got a touch of cystitis.'

A 'touch', trying to trivialise it, but it blighted the whole day like a bad weather forecast.

'Aaw, poor you! Did you bring anything for it?'

'No. I'll get something today. Come on, you'll be late.'

While Iain showered I shook the creases from our clothes, listened to

Blue Danube Radio, your English-language station in Vienna!

The music was easy listening, making me grind my teeth. Requests for retired ex-pats, favourite tunes for Golden Weddings. I hadn't heard a southern English accent for four years, and the DJ's voice seemed ludicrous, a parody, Pythonesque.

'No-one speaks like that!' I said it aloud to hear my own, real voice.

There was a jingle: gentle, instrumental, and

the international news after this break.

I turned it off, wanting to stay news free for a while, in tourist limbo.

In the breakfast room, Iain grabbed a Danish pastry to eat on the way. I stayed longer, lingering over pots of tea: hot stainless steel that scalded my fingers, the teabags on strings, lying like drowned mice in the saucer. I avoided the grapefruit juice; just the thought of it turned to needles in my abdomen. I wanted a deep, warm bath, to soak like a hippopotamus with only my eyes showing, but there was no tub in our room. Instead, I got the name of an English-speaking doctor from the receptionist and went out into the squinting sunshine to find his surgery.

There was nothing fresh about the morning, just the wearying weight of heat. I hopped over tram lines, imagined my foot caught in one, the tram coming towards me while people screamed through the windows. A disaster! An item on the news. It could never happen.

The street names were impossibly long. My tourist's map got creased and re-creased, faded at the folds, and I had to stop every few minutes. The German words, lists of nouns, slid away from my brain, slipped my grasp. I circled my destination in pencil and made it by following lefts and rights.

I couldn't find 'cystitis' in the phrase book, but they had 'bladder'. I said it, 'Die Blase, ss-ss!', miming pain, and the receptionist indicated that I should sit and wait.

Half an hour passed. The waiting room filled with happy sick people, whole families of them. Malingering children bounced robustly on their mothers' laps. They all went in ahead of me and I began to wonder if I had been overlooked. It was hot. Sitting by the window, the sun painting my arm and face. So hot.

I tipped my head back, felt the sweat cool on my neck; a rivulet ran down and pooled on my breast bone. My legs felt fat, clammy, they stuck together under my damp cotton skirt. A loose thread at my shoulder tickled and itched, and I pulled at it, twisted it around until my finger bulged with blood, but the stubborn nylon wouldn't snap. An hour and a half. Two hours. I clung to my chair, riding the pain, desperately wanting the toilet but scared to lose my place. Surely it couldn't be much longer? What if they'd called my name but pronounced it wrong so that I hadn't heard? I chewed down the panic and closed my eyes.

The sun on my face.

Miss Gabriel's voice, bright:

'And the wolf was *so* greedy, he swallowed the little goat whole!'

which sounds like The End, but it can't be; my class mates, cross-legged on the floor, look as worried as I am.

'Then he lay down under a shady tree to sleep off his meal. Well, the goat's mother heard her son bleating, still alive inside the wolf! She took her sewing scissors and she snip! snipped! the wolf's stomach open. The little goat jumped out, as happy as could be. Then the goat's mother took her needle and thread, and she sewed up a rock in the wolf's tummy.'

The frightening illustration in the book: the wolf sweating, his eyes glazed and bulging, lurching to the river to drink.

'The rock in his belly was so heavy that it toppled him into the water, and he was Never. Seen. Again!'

I felt the rock in my belly, the weight dragging down. I was a Bosch creature, a bladder on legs, the bladder on fire. A man's voice said my name. He said it perfectly, pouring out the words like water. I opened my eyes to see the doctor's face, and peeled my legs from the chair.

The patient, a British woman in her twenties, burst into tears upon entering the office. After some time, we were able to establish that the symptoms indicated cystitis and that the patient is an habitual sufferer. Prescription:

He rummaged in his desk drawer, through lengths of rubber tubing and metal instruments, a glove, sunglasses, sweets, a tub of yellow pills. He counted the pills out with his pen into a sheet of paper, and folded it to make an envelope.

'Three times a day,' he said. 'Avoid alcohol, don't drive, don't get pregnant.'

'As if!' I gave him a sorry grin. 'Can I ask what they are?'

'No.'

The consultation cost three hundred and sixty schillings. He stuffed the money into the drawer and escorted me out through the waiting room, kind now where he had been brisk before. Curious faces followed me as I left, shaky and red-eyed. I hoped they thought I'd had terrible news.

Back at the hotel, with the sun winkling through the loose-weaved orange curtains, I took two of the yellow pills to catch up, and slept naked on top of the covers. I dreamt of water, clear, cold bottles of it, twinkling and spinning, and an angel in a turquoise bather who swam around my head, although I swatted her. Vast circles swelled and spread like cine-film on fire, and ate little circles who couldn't get away; so greedy that they swallowed them whole.

Iain came in just after five o'clock and woke me.

'God, it's hot! How are you?'

I thought about it.

'A bit better. I had the weirdest dreams, though. I think I'm high; I went to the doctor and he gave me mysterious pills.'

'Junkie.' He unpacked the lap-top from a nylon bag with the conference logo on the side. 'There's another one from Danielle.'

> Hi, guys! I wish I was with you there, everything is quiet here. I got my hairs cut. Stéphane hates it, but he is dumb. You ask who is Levin. He sends e-mail to everyone, it's LONG, he says they're stealing his work and they won't give him tenure. It is War and Peace here and Levin is the War. Maybe he will go back to Russia and it will be peaceful. We plan to make a barbecue soon, but maybe after you are back. I got a cute dress pattern from *Vogue*, with short sleeves for summer, so I am always sewing now. Keep having fun.

Danielle kneeling on the living-room floor, pins in her mouth, cutting a paper pattern tacked to cloth. Everything symmetrical, fronts to backs. Her apartment is decorated in cool greens and blues; in the evening light, it's like being underwater. Before dinner, she swam around her kitchen, happily burning dish-cloths.

'You're the clumsiest person I know!'

'Oo cares!'

Now she measures her dressmaking on the floor, missing the edges, so her carpet looks like the scene of a murder: chalk outlines of bodies, no heads.

> Danielle, it is still hot but at least there is no snow, eh. I have cystitis, boo hoo, but I have drugs for it, hooray. I am being the total tourist, seeing all the sights, eating all the cakes. The galleries are wonderful. On the last night of the conference, we are going to a Reception at the Museum of Twentieth-century

Art. It's a funny old century to be in a museum already! I'll send you a postcard of the worst and best paintings. Big hug.

Leaning back on the bed, stretching out, something chimed against my fingers and I was soaked in water.

'The glass! Look what you're doing!'

'I'm sorry! I'm sorry! I don't think there's any on the computer . . .'

He snatched it from me and held it aloft, looking for drips.

'Christ! Can't you be more careful? That's it; you're not using it again.'

'I'm sorry.'

The pillow was wet and there was a dark line on the sheet where the water had dripped between my legs. I righted the glass.

'Look, there's still some in it; I can't have spilled much.' But we were both annoyed by the suddenness of it.

A bronze dragon lay flat beneath the Anker Clock, hunting it, or guarding it, his jaws dripping green age. Above was the sun-face of the clock, a laughing cherub to one side, what looked like a skull to the other. Perhaps the clock was Heaven and the dragon was Hell. People in the crowd creased their guide books open to the page with the Anker Clock, looked up at it and told each other the time in English, French, German.

'Midi moins cinq.'

'Not long now.'

An old man pushed through the crowd, but pushed without touching anyone; we parted for him like a sea. He wore a stained sheet as a toga, a wreath on his head that he had made from real leaves, touchingly tatty and inept. His skin was mottled and loose, the elasticity lost, scarred by sun and age. He carried a staff with a cardboard cut-out apple on it: a delicious picture, red, as big as a football with a drawn-on window of shine. With his arms raised like wings, he blessed the crowd, beatific, calm. And he united us. We began catching each other's eyes, grinning, the international code: ah, a nutter! But a nutter with a purpose. He had a sign around his neck, '*Ewig*', and a smaller text underneath.

I couldn't find the word in my phrase book. I took a photograph of him, but only when he wasn't looking; if he really were an angel, perhaps he wouldn't show on film.

An American boy pushed his girlfriend forward.

'Lisa! Turn him this way! Put your arm around him.'

Lisa, tall and very human, reached out to touch his shoulder. His face morphed from angel to devil, and he spat at her, an angry, wet mark on the shoulder of her T-shirt. The staff swung in his fists, the red apple bobbing and spinning, round, flat, round.

'Hey, you fucken' moron! What the hell are you doing?'

Lisa ducked and ran. The crowd pulled back, leaving a discreet circle where the angel swore and sparred in a fury that had seized him like a fit, and the Americans moved to the front of the crowd, nonchalant, making it look as if they'd intended it. On the Anker Clock, medieval characters paraded in blue and gold: knights, ladies and peasants, as stiff and posed as playing cards. The midday show had begun and no-one had noticed.

Danielle's house. She shows us around before we start to help her move. Her husband has already taken his belongings; there are nails spattering the walls, the pale, rectangular ghosts of pictures, lengths of dust on the skirting where his furniture used to be. In the kitchen is a big American fridge with a drinks dispenser, but that has been sold with the house, and it stands dark and ajar, an empty sarcophagus without its soul of electricity.

Iain, Dave and Stéphane move the heavy pieces, pretending that they're light, toughing it out. Danielle and I do the folding and packing, put books into boxes. New Age, astrology, a manual: 'Votre Machine à Coudre Singer'. I wave *Your Psychic Workout* at her:

'I *knew* you were going to bring this!'

'Oh, you make me laugh too much!'

She snatches it from me, Scotch tape flapping from her wrists and elbows, and stuffs it in alongside her bad-taste posters: basking walruses groaning about Mondays, kittens pledging friendship to red-bowed puppies. There are no photographs of her husband, and Iain and I have never seen him. The Danielle we know is a single package.

She drives the rental van like a tank. Sitting in the front with her, on the wrong side, I phantom-drive; reaching to change gear, wincing when oncoming cars pass us on the left, convinced that we are all playing 'chicken'. I can hear the guys yelling in the back, something or someone sliding across the floor as Danielle takes a corner. We unload the van at her new apartment and drive back to Laval for more.

How Danielle's house was built:

They bought the plot and dug the foundations. They chose their house from a builder's yard, and it arrived on a lorry in two halves, like an Easter egg. They dropped the halves into the foundations, focused them into place, and joined the nerves and arteries, the plumbing and wiring, bringing the two parts together. The builders left, the muddy path they had trodden in the lawn began to grow back, and Danielle and her husband were left alone to begin the task of breaking up their marriage.

She takes us to the basement for a last look.

'See, that's where they joined it together. If you take out these bolts – bof! It falls into pieces!'

The bolts, each the size of a fist, form a seam up the walls and over our heads. We all have to touch them, pretend to turn them, imagine it. It would be the ultimate practical joke on the next occupants. Something in Danielle's expression makes me say, 'Don't even think it!'

Bright-eyed, she pushes her hair back and puffs her cheeks. We have tried to keep things light all day, considering her feelings, but she is excited and eager for change. Her real personality is better than any front I could put on.

She brings out her camera.

'Goodbye photograph!'

We pose against the wall, arms contorted. She loves it.

'Wall Art!' Snap snap.

'One with Danielle in!'

Dave takes it. Danielle is too worked up to stand still, and, when she gets the film developed two months later, she is just a blur: dancing denim and black hair. Snap. But she is settled into her underwater apartment by then, and we have our own place in the West End, and we feel like we have known each other forever.

The reception at the Museum of Twentieth-century Art. Waiters offered trays of drinks, champagne and orange juice. Thinking of the yellow pills, I chose the juice. Valéry, the Russian professor who had dogged us from the bus, took two glasses of champagne and tried to make me drink one, his arm tight around my shoulder. I considered spitting on him.

'Back off, man; I'm packing a urinary tract infection!'

I said it quickly so that he wouldn't understand, but in any case he laughed heartily in my face, alcohol and onions. I asked him if he knew the lecturer who was sending the long e-mails back in Montreal, but he said: 'Levin? Pah, it is a common name.'

I shrugged his hand from my shoulder and stared at the paintings, then closed my eyes to make their complementary colours burn on my retinas: red for green, yellow for purple. I looked at the people looking at the paintings. There was a method to it: stand close up, then step elaborately back. Look like you're musing, then nod with understanding. If you've got a beard, stroke it.

Valéry pushed his face close to mine.

'I think they hung them upside-down, ha ha!'

'I wish they'd hang *you* upside-down,' I said, and he laughed uproariously, turning heads. His voice floated upwards with the others, joined the ceiling of sound. These huge, high rooms in show-off Vienna, everything gilded and intricate, built by rich men like some favour to the world. Then the contrast of the modern works: squares of colour that spoke to each other, a line drawn large and long, like a memory. It made the people look small and insufficient, flawed. I wanted to sheepdog-chase them all out then walk back through the silent halls alone, rippling the silence like the first person in a swimming pool. I struck out for the waiters at the top of the staircase, ducked between bodies, and lost Valéry.

'Do you have any water?'

The waiter looked like a student, young, a little disdainful of his white apron and red waistcoat. His eyes flickered briefly, translating the request, and he searched in the crates beneath the tablecloth.

'Perrier?' Holding up a party-sized bottle of it.

'That'll do, thanks.'

He diapered it ironically in white linen, treating it like champagne, turning the bottle instead of the cap. There were beads of sweat on the glass. I felt a lurch of thirst in my throat at the sight of them: the green globules outside, the bubbles inside. If I closed my eyes, the bottle would be a pale, transparent red. The cap was tight. The waiter firmed his mouth, shifted his grasp, and forced it free with a metallic crick. He gave a small frown, and the bottle squirmed out of the napkin like a cat. We saw the thick glass base appear, raised our hands to it together; our fingers brushed lightly, and the bottle fell and hit the first step.

Impact.

A loud crack, silencing the room.

The bottle, unbroken, tilted over the first step and rolled down, gathered speed, spitting and spinning, a fizzing gush on the wide, white marble, too beautiful and terrible to stop, with a relentless, bulleting sound each time that threatened to split the glass but didn't

bang
    bang
        bang
            bang
                bang

until a waiter coming up the stairs stopped it with his foot, a relief and a disappointment. After the silence, everyone spoke at once and, standing at the top of the echoing staircase, I could have drowned in the noise.

The night-shift receptionist said that '*ewig*' meant 'eternal', with no curiosity as to why I had asked. She yawned and wished us

'Good night', returned to her magazine. We made a terrific tiptoeing to our room, locked the door thunderously with the clumsy plastic key. Iain turned on

Blue Danube Radio

and I flopped on the bed, groaning.

'No!'

bringing you the international news after this break

'I don't want to hear the news; I'm on holiday!'

'I'm not! I'm working.' He cracked open the lap-top, a box of light in the dark room. We were drunk and hot enough to argue about it, but too tired. I turned over and spoke into the pillow.

'Yeah, but it's not too bad, working in Vienna. A bit different . . .'

Mitchell University in Montreal, Canada

'Hush a minute! It's Mitchell!'

'What?'

a shooting rampage in the Department of Engineering that left two dead and three others critically injured. The gunman was eventually overpowered by a security guard and is now in police custody. He has been named as Constantine Levin, a professor said to have held a grudge against the University.

And finally, tomorrow's weather . . .

We waited, listening for more news, but for everyone else the night was moving on to

a medley of songs from the shows!

'E-mail,' said Iain quietly, reaching for the keyboard; but his hands trembled too much and he let me take the lap-top from him without a word.

I tapped in a message, pressed a button to send it. My thoughts had already flown on ahead.

I am walking down the corridor, past the doors of people who have become our friends, whose accents we don't hear any more.

Then Iain's name plate.

I trace the letters with my finger, hesitating on the second 'i'.

Below it is a notice, 'I will be in Vienna until . . .' and below that, a smiley face, drawn there by Danielle.

I want to knock at Danielle's door, but I am afraid that she won't be in.

High Five

i. Flying Blind

'ARE YOU WEARING CLEAN underpants?' says Gramps, not for the first time. He chuckles like hydraulics and winches his knees wider, wider, until I am flattened against the bus window, my hair making feathery fronds in the wet glass. Inside his voluminous trousers, he has Mr Dolls' House legs: pipe-cleaner thin, with knots for knees. His feet are tortoised in heavy shoes, which fall in odd places, as random and dangerous as logs tumbling from a fire. Timmy whines and scrambles on to my lap to escape.

'Of course, the first thing you'll do in the event of a crash is wet yourself,' Gramps adds, and my father looks round from the seat in front:

'Are you scaring that kid?'

'Indeed, no!' But when my father turns back, he whispers, 'In addition, you may soil yourself. Not much point in clean underpants after all!'

He taps a 'punchline' rhythm on the back of my mother's seat.

'Ba-diddley dum!'

My mother has confiscated his walking stick to stop him going up and down the bus. He has been shaking people's hands and telling them 'Goodbye' with such solemn finality that Mrs Beynon says:

'Come on, Joe! It's only a holiday. We'll be back in ten days.'

'I'll always remember you like this,' he replies. 'So happy and hopeful!'

He's not supposed to be on the bus anyway. It's a charter, part of the package for our Spanish trip. But he knows the driver. He knows Everybody.

And Everybody is on the bus. Travel mania has hit our village like a summer fashion. I imagine the streets are empty now, dust blowing against the blank windows, and weeds springing on the lawns, knee-deep. Vernon the Bread is on the bus with his roly-poly wife, and Dai Butcher is sitting at the front with a sombrero on – cows and sheep dance with relief in the fields. Our bachelor Minister sits on the long pew at the back, between his two sisters. They go everywhere together, Cerberus-like, to stop the Minister getting led astray by women. He is eighty-nine years old and the experience would surely kill him. Now the few non-travellers of his congregation will have to sit on their sins for the next ten days in the vacated village.

'The robbers will have a field day,' said Gramps, so I have brought a handbag of treasures: my blonde Pippa doll, and her dusky sister Marie, like a Before and After of me in the Spanish sun. I have the key to the box that I hope one day to find, and the swathe of skin that I peeled off my brother's back a sunburnt summer ago, folded like a veil and tucked into a thimble.

David has been made to sit by Mandy Evans. To look out of the window would be to crick his neck in her direction, so he stares down at his lap instead and twists his Action Man into strange and brutal poses. Mandy – a sophisticated and voracious thirteen – can get no information from my brother, other than that his favourite band is 'Shut up!' and that the team he supports is also called 'Shut up!' He would no sooner talk to a girl than his Action Man would play with my dolls. (But hah! When he is at rugby practice, Action Man takes Pippa and Marie to the Shoe-box Disco in his tank. He has Eagle Eyes, Gripping Hands and Dancing Feet.)

We drive under a bridge, and Timmy has a go at his sudden reflection in the window. I try to huss him on to the squashed, furry patties on the road, but he doesn't recognise them as rabbits at all. He yelps a scale, his prehistoric mouth full of pink and black gums, and a thread of saliva abseils from his tongue, leaving wirey slug trails on my skirt.

'I don't know why we brought that stinking dog!' snaps my mother over her shoulder.

'Marilyn Monroe had a poodle called Maff,' says Gramps, apropos of nothing. 'Horrible dogs, mind. It's a prostitute's dog, is a poodle.' He spits into his handkerchief. 'She had it stuffed when it died,' he lies.

Timmy starts to squirm on my lap, throwing his arthritic hips about in an agitated samba. He flings one cracked, walker's paw into the air.

'Oh no! Gramps, Timmy wants a wee!'

'Comfort Stop!' yells Gramps. 'Comfort Stop for the dog!'

We're hardly out of the town yet, not even on the motorway.

'We could still put him off,' my mother tells my father. 'Someone would be bound to pick him up and take him back.'

Gramps is shocked.

'I'm not have Timmy hitch-hiking like a vagrant!'

'Not him,' she says. 'You.'

Everyone yells 'Airport!' as we pass the sign.

'Cardiff Wales Airport,' adds Gramps more precisely. 'There's a curse on the airfield, the people say.'

The bus trembles and whines to a halt, and the smokers on board make a rush for the door. The Minister's sisters frogmarch him out, to stop him touching any women, and stand him at a safe distance while they unload their massive trunk.

'This isn't Barry Island,' he says.

'You're going to Spain,' Gramps reminds him.

'That's right!' The Minister beams. 'It's colder than I thought, mind.' He gazes out over the expanse of car park like a heron on an estuary. Mrs Beynon approaches him tremulously, with a wobbly will that she wrote on the bus, and Gramps draws me to one side.

'You'll be catered for spiritually in a crash,' he says. 'The

Minister can pray for your perishing souls.' He claps his hand on my head like a man catching a rugby ball. 'Ah, you are but a spotless child!'

But I'm covered in drool and dog hairs, and only by jumping away from Timmy, who is peeing against the bus tyre, do I manage to save my shoes. Gramps does a clog dance around the piddle and attaches a lead to Timmy's collar; Timmy goes into a crazy whirl, maypoling the lead around Gramps' walking stick.

'They won't let you take *him* in!' says my mother.

Gramps studies the sky, the birds wheeling and cawing overhead.

'Gulls!' he says. 'They fly into the engines . . . have you got your passports? They'll need the passports to identify your bodies.'

My father clutches at his heart, but he's just checking the tickets. He has loaded his pockets with all the things he might need if Spain is hit by nuclear war, and he waddles in his wide trousers. His money jingles like spurs as he drags the biggest suitcase. Its wheels weep with each step of the long journey from the bus park, and at intervals it falls on its side like a horse that's died of exhaustion. The bus driver helps the Minister's sisters to drag their trunk, which is the size of a sofa and the weight of a piano; they look like they're off to build a pyramid with it. The Minister follows on with his little spade.

'For sand,' he says.

On the airport's glass door there is a 'No Dogs' sign, a black terrier struck by red lightning.

'I told you!' My mother pokes the sign.

'Why'd they say "Except Guide Dogs"?' asks my brother in a fit of logic. 'Blind people can't see that it's "No Dogs" can they?'

Gramps changes the subject.

'Did you remember your sunglasses?'

'Sunglasses? Yeah . . .'

'Give us a go, eh?' He badgers my brother, tugs at his arm. 'Give us a go of your sunglasses, boy.'

'Yuhawright.'

Gramps levers them on to his face and starts tapping about with his stick.

'Oh no, Dad – that's disgusting!'

'Awright Gramps!'

My mother grabs him by the lapels and snarls into his face:

'You'll be sorry, you old weasel! I'll put you in the Blind Home when we get back!'

'I'll hitch-hike there myself,' he says mildly. 'Come on Timmy, lead the way.'

It's not how I imagined it, trawling my bank of 'airport' images. Less glamorous than in the films. Richard Burton is not here with Elizabeth Taylor. There is no newsreel man who has in his hand a piece of paper, no singing nuns. There aren't even any terrorists, only a coach trip from Bargoed, tough as cowboys around the sandwich bar.

The British Citizens of the village take out their passports, panicking the Minister with the solemn blue covers.

'No no! I'm on holiday – see?' He waves the little spade. His sisters show him his passport to explain, but they won't trust him to hold it. His photograph looks like the seat was missing from the *Photo Me* booth; only a spike left, his hair a shocked halo around his head.

Our Family Passport doesn't include David and me, just our Baader–Meinhoff parents. Careful of the cost, they took turns to jump in and out of the booth between flashes, while David and I stood blushing in the Post Office.

'If we lost it, we couldn't go,' says my mother wistfully.

'Think of the expense!' says my father.

'If you lost it out there, you couldn't come back,' says Gramps, and my mother drops her case on the floor. She gets maximum gravity out of it, the sound slapping around the airport's shabby walls.

'Listen, you . . .' she tells Gramps.

David grabs my arm: 'Uh oh! Here it comes!' And we start edging away, because my mother has had a tantrum waiting in the wings for some time, and now it looks like it is stepping out into the spotlight.

For the past two weeks, my mother has been Not Going, because she fears getting strip-searched at Security. Every night, I lay awake, thinking of Spanish bulls and senoritas and castanets, wondering what it was about castanets that was vaguely rude, and worried now that I would never find out. By day, my mother washed and ironed our clothes, all the time muttering 'Filthy!' and 'Perverts!' and 'Lesbians get jobs at the airport just so they can do it!' She couldn't see a pair of rubber gloves without bursting into tears. But she boiled her underwear in a thick elastic soup on the stove, and wouldn't let us wear the clean clothes, so I figured we were going after all.

Now she stamps an angry fandango at my Gramps and unleashes all the tension of the last two weeks, all her fear of flying.

'You nasty, *nasty* old man! You're winding *me* up! You're winding those poor *kids* up!' She points at us, and we're too scared to shake our heads. 'You drag that revolting dog everywhere you're not invited, and all you can do is make stupid remarks. You're useless. *Useless*!'

Gramps hangs his head. Everything is quiet. Then one of the Bargoed coach trip drawls:

'Aw, pity! And he's blind too!'

My mother lets out a small scream and rushes off to the toilets.

Gramps and my father exchange looks; Action Man hangs his head. I reach for my comforting handbag and realise that I have left it on the bus.

'Dad!'

'You'll just have to leave it.'

'Da–ad!'

'I said *leave it*, Becca!' He pulls his hands from his pockets and his money scatters as if he did it on purpose: sterling to the left, pesetas to the right. 'Look at me! I'm panicking!' He kneels to grab at the scrabbling coins.

This trip is rotten. I already hate it. But David surprises me by turning up with the bus key, showing it to me in a quick uncurl of his hand.

'I asked the driver. But we have to be *quick*. Come on.'

Our shoes squeak on the rubberised floor of the airport, through the glass door, and out on to the tarmac. The buses are so far away that they look like a mirage, blocks of sunlight shining on their roofs. I start to whimper, but David grabs my hand and hauls me along behind him. 'Run! Run!' We dodge through the car park; the mirrors brush my head, wiping me with traffic grime, and I see flashes of other people's cars with toys in the back and the odd shocked dog, and stickers from Longleat, St Fagan's Museum, Cheddar Gorge. Sensible places, places you can do in a day with a bag of Opal Fruits and a Thermos and no-one shouting.

We come to a bus that looks like ours, but it has just arrived, its engine still hot and coughing. Strange people are getting out, strange smokers lighting up outside. The children stare at us territorially. We try the next one, but the key won't fit, and besides, it's bigger, smarter. What were we thinking? There are ten more buses here, and a sign for a secondary bus park further away, like a Dinky garage in the distance.

'Oh . . . *bloody*!' says David.

'They won't go without us though, will they?'

'No. They'll only have to miss the *plane*. We're only going to get *killed*.'

I feel moisture like a touch on the back of my leg, warm then cool. I haven't wet myself in years, not since baby school. But I reach down and feel ticklish whiskers, and it's Timmy! Timmy is licking my leg!

'Timmy!' I grab the greasy ruff of his neck, and then Gramps comes tapping into view.

'We fancied a little walk,' he says, to save David's pride. 'And look, Timmy followed your trail! Good dog!'

Gramps carries my handbag over his arm, making me laugh.

'I'm just an old woman!' he quavers.

'Hee hee!'

'I'm just an old woman out for a walk!'

But he hides it behind his back as we approach the terminal and see Dai Butcher's sombrero, pansying in the window.

These are the people from my village, lined up like their own terraced houses. The Minister has dug his way to the front of the queue, and stands amid an angelic flutter of stewardesses. His monumental sisters clasp their handbags to their hearts and pray for a room with no view. Dai Butcher is sandwiched between Vernon and Mrs Vernon in a conspiracy of shopkeepers. Their pockets ring with money fresh from the till; floured pounds and cow-brown pennies. Mandy Evans shoots looks at the Bargoed cowboys until her vigilante parents rope her in. My five-foot mother seems tall and strong next to Mrs Beynon's fifteen jellying stones, and my father has counted himself into submission with the contents of his pockets. My brother and I are holiday-happy, dancing; the next time I go to the toilet, it will be in the air!

Gramps brings out his camera.

'Say "cheese"!'

'There's sweet,' coos a stewardess. 'I suppose he can tell where you are from your voices.'

Gramps asks her to stand with us, 'Because you sound so pretty!' he tells her chest. He points and clicks, winds on the film with a ratcheting noise.

'To remember you by!'

But I know he has beheaded us all; his photograph albums are littered with anonymous bodies.

In his dark glasses, in his jaunty hat, he looks like an old Bluesman. As we start to file through, he pulls out his handkerchief and waves us Goodbye, and the last thing I see as I go through the gate is my handbag swinging merrily on his arm.

ii. Eating Paris

THE RED LIGHT WENT on and David counted hippopotamuses. Not enough hippos, and she wouldn't have spent long enough, maybe wouldn't have washed her hands. Too many, and she would be doing something that he didn't want to think about too deeply, getting a big seat-smile on her buttocks . . . whoa! He reined the thought in, and sent the hippos into slo-mo, a graceful *Fantasia* dance, aware that he was cheating. But it was okay. The light went out in a respectable eighty hippos, and Miss Rose came out of the toilet, shaking her hands. *A washer*! He'd known she would be.

He and Howie tensed in frozen yearning as she brushed past their seat, sashaying her hips in the slim aisle. They groaned as she turned sideways and Benson oozed past her, advancing on them in a wobbly prowl, nicotined fingers clawing the headrests. Booze patrol. The stewardesses had been warned.

'Boys.'

'All right, sir? Want a peanut?'

'A moveable feast, eh! Thanks, Howie.'

He formed his yellow fingers into a beak, dabbled them in the silvery bag. They came out powdered with dry roasting, a peanut pincered in the fingertips, and he sucked it into his mouth.

'Now, I'm telling all you boys, right – no drinking, no wacky-baccy, and leave "les girls" alone. Don't want you getting stabbed by a French pimp. Not on school time anyway.'

The bit about maturity and trust now . . .

'We're trusting you, mind. You're mature enough to know how to behave.'

'Yes, sir.'

Benson's fags made a shape in his shirt pocket; he kept touching them, couldn't wait to get off the plane and light up.

'Not sitting with your sister, David?'

'Aw, sir, mun!'

'Right, well; remember what I said.' He moved on and they heard him at the next row: 'Now, I'm telling all the boys . . .'

Howie flipped a peanut at David.

'For why'd you bring your sister, Dai?'

'I didn't bring her, right! She *came*.' He shook his head. 'Look, this is me, earning this trip: *swot swot swot, wash the car David, mow the lawn David*! And this is my sister, *earning* this trip: *please Daddy, please Daddy, please please please*!' He bounced up and down in his seat.

'Phew!' said Howie. 'Glad I've only got a dog.'

'We got a dog too,' said David glumly.

Howie glanced over his shoulder. 'Never mind; look.' He opened his jacket. The curved shoulder of a bottle nestled in the pocket.

'Whisky! Where'd you get that?'

'Ssh-ut *up*! My dad. For passing my exams.'

'Yeah, that's another thing! All this stuff they promise you to pass your exams – like you'd go and fail otherwise. Like you wouldn't bother!'

'Easy, Davey boy! Have a peanut.' Bouncing one off him.

'I mean, *my* exams! They're *mine*! I don't need a *reward*. Ah, stop it Howie.'

'Boing!'

'Howie, stop it.'

'Baa-ding!'

'Oi! Those are *my* peanuts!'

David grabbed him by the throat and throttled him against the window, popping his head in and out of the deep oval frame, rattling the plastic pane.

'Bloody hell, Dai!' Howie struggled free and rubbed his ears. 'Relaxez-vous! You need a holiday, you do.'

David sat back and tried to stretch, but his feet were too big, his Doc Martens in danger of getting wedged under the seat in front. He often felt constrained by his body; felt that he had grown inside during the night, and that, if only he could stretch enough, he would burst out of himself, fingers folding back like ears of corn to make way for the new fingers inside him. It was a constant itching at his seams, making him fidget, making the teachers tell him off in class.

He tuned in to Miss Rose's humming-bird voice at the front of the plane. She was giving the pep talk to the First Year girls. He would ask her a question later, something intelligent about France, to impress her, to hear her say his name.

'You're more mature than the boys,' she was saying.

'Come over here, Miss!' Howie snickered; '*I'm* mature! Ow! Dai, mun!'

Paris smelt of perfume. He hadn't expected that. Everyone had said that it would smell of drains, of garlic, but no. It was the particular essence of sun meeting city: late summer flowers and smoky urban grass. Even the car fumes were different, exotic. He breathed it in, logging it as a memory, better than a photograph. Miss Rose had a poster of the Eiffel Tower in class, an aerial shot of the splayed 'A'. A cliché. But up close, you could use all your senses to make it your own. He focused in on the nearest girder: *I'm touching the Eiffel Tower.* It was brown, not black. He closed his eyes to hear the backdrop of sounds, voices and traffic in an arcing echo; pressed his face to the metal and felt the texture with his tongue. *This is me licking the Eiffel Tower.* He was certain that no-one else had ever licked the Eiffel Tower.

Howie wanted to pee off the top. No imagination.

His sister tapped his shoulder.

'What you doing?'

'I'm licking the Eiffel Tower. Go away.'

'I want to lick it too!'

'Nuh. Go away, Becca.'

'I want to! I want to lick the Eiffel Tower! Let me–e–e!'

He held her at arm's length. 'Hmm – yum yum! It tastes of chocolate!'

'I'm telling Mammy!'

Horror-voiced: 'Your Mammy isn't here now, little girl.'

'I'll tell Miss, then.'

But the teachers were off in the distance, relaxed. Benson was playing football with some foreign kids, coughing and gobbing. Miss Rose was eating sorbet from a tub, licking the plastic spoon with a dreamy, creamy look on her face. He'd been surprised and relieved to hear her speak French; in class, he'd had the unworthy suspicion that she wouldn't be able to hack it in France, that she was only two steps ahead of the pupils. But she was great. Her mouth made sweet shapes as she complained to the proprietor about the hostel toilets, waving her arms, pursing her lips. It was like watching your parents at a party, the moment when they leap to their feet and start jiving expertly.

Howie appeared at the far side of the green, looking furtive. David watched as he dipped into a mad, low gallop, running like Groucho, trying to sneak unnoticed across the open space. His arms were cuddled across a large white carrier bag, hiding it uselessly against his chest. He pulled up abruptly, willing himself invisible, and peeked out behind an air-tree; and then he was off again, running erratically left and right, with the wide, wild curves of a coursed hare, his body upright and his legs pedalling frantically below him. Closer, five feet away, and he stopped.

'Invisible Spy Man!' he yelled, then, 'Hush! It's only me.' There was whisky on his breath.

'What you got there, Howie?'

He held up the carrier bag. 'They sold me wine in the shop! Didn't ask, just sold me it!'

'Yeah?'

'Yeah, party tonight! Par-*tay*! Come on, you can get some too, it's just over there.'

On the previous nights, they had stayed in the hostel's games room, where Miss Rose challenged all-comers to vigorous bouts of table tennis.

'Nah, don't think I'll bother.'

'All right then, we'll break out after dark and find a bar – pick up a couple of girls. Improve your *French*!' Howie wagged his tongue, lewd.

David thought of it. A girl like Pascale in their French book. Long hair that curled up at the shoulder, and a stripey sweater with things happening perkily underneath it. She would talk in speech bubbles, tell him where to find the *église* and the *hôtel de ville*. He'd take her to a café and name all the crockery on the table. Masculine and feminine.

'Mm. Maybe.'

But that night, after dinner, Howie was sick, and the next morning he was worse.

'Hangover!' pronounced Benson with distaste.

Miss Rose put her hand on Howie's forehead.

'Oh, Howell!'

David glared at him over her shoulder, but Howie was grey, sour and malt-smelling, couldn't take advantage of his position.

'You spoil it for everyone,' said Benson. 'Miss Rose will have to stay and look after you now.'

'Me? Why not you?'

They haggled, tossed for it, then couldn't agree which side of the French money was 'heads'. They did scissors–paper–stone, and Miss Rose lost.

'All right then. But David will have to go with his sister. If you take my boys, he can keep an eye on the First Year girls.'

'*Miss*!'

'Listen to Miss Rose!' Benson was relieved, backing her up to allay his guilt.

David spelt out a sentence in gestures to Howie:

I – KILL – YOU!

Howie signalled back to him with his eyes:

PLEASE! DO!

* * *

'The Louvre!' he said. 'Haven't you ever heard of the Louvre?'

The girls blinked up at him, did it together like Midwich Cuckoos.

'He said *loofah*! Hee hee!'

'My mother's got a loofah,' said one of them. 'In her toilet.'

'She said *toilet*!'

'That's not a loofah, it's just a museum. We can tell.'

'That's just the way in,' he said. 'There's paintings inside, of, you know, ponies and things. Come on, it'll be brilliant.'

But he couldn't move them. They ignored him with superb effectiveness, as if his voice were something that they could simply tune out. He couldn't even threaten them; they'd start to cry. Or they'd jump him; there were enough of them. He felt overwhelmed, ineffectual. Was this what it was like to be a teacher?

'Come on, please! Miss Rose said that I have to take you there!'

'Nuh-huh.'

'Don't wanna go.'

'What do you want to do then?' He tried to think what he normally did with his sister, but he couldn't start fighting with her in the middle of Paris. 'Where d'you want to go?'

They sang in chorus:

'SHOPPING!'

He took them to Galeries Lafayette, and they tried on the same clothes as each other, twittering in and out of the changing rooms in reds and purples and bright pinks. Little girl colours.

'How much? How much?'

He translated the prices from francs to pounds and they swore like sailors. While they changed, he fingered a rack of Lacoste shirts, and eyed the sales girls shyly. The sun streamed through the wide windows, piercing the city grime; it seemed to consume time, moved across the sky with greedy speed. One day in Paris, happening outside without him. Not that he'd wanted a reward, but *this*! It wasn't fair.

'This is my holiday!' he said aloud. '*Mes vacances*!'

'*M'sieur?*' A sales girl approached, waved a bottle. She was offering to spray him with cologne. He nodded, held out his wrist as he had seen his mother do; but the girl shook her head. Moving in close, she hooked the tip of her finger into his shirt collar and drew it gently down. He closed his eyes. A little hushing sound, and a cool wetness that dried quickly on the soft, hot skin of his neck. He opened his eyes again. The girl gave him a confidential smile, touched his collar back into place, and was gone. He felt as if he'd been kissed.

When the girls came back out, he was dazed, stared at them.

'Everything's too expensive!'

'It's dear!' An old-fashioned word, picked up from a parent. *Dear*, he thought. *Cher. Chèrie.*

His sister took his hand and swung it, showing off: *my big brother*.

'David!' she said, 'We're hungry! Hungre–e–e!'

They nodded in unison, skipped on the spot like anxious chorus girls.

'Yeah, right.' He dug out the tourist map that Miss Rose had given him. 'Did you know they have McDonald's in France?'

'HOORAY!'

They walked back singing, arm in arm, stepping into their own long shadows, made even more coltish by the low sun. Just before it closed, they caught a sweet shop that sold sugar models of Parisian landmarks. The assistant wrapped them separately, elaborately, in dainty boxes with curling ribbons, and the girls ripped them open on the pavement outside, scoffing the contents; crunchy little Eiffel Towers and Arcs de Triomphe. Eating Paris. For himself, he bought a sugared wafer with the Mona Lisa printed crudely on it – the nearest that he would get now – and, on a second thought, bought another one for Miss Rose. He would give it to her when they got back. He was pleased that he'd thought of it himself.

He organised the tickets for the Métro, did a head count in whispered increments of two. They were quiet now, slouched in their seats, heads poised sweetly on each other's shoulders while the movement of the train rocked them. His sister shoogled down into the seat beside him.

'David! I got blisters!' She took her sandals off to show him.

'Hmm.'

'What do I do now?'

'Soak them in salt water when you get back.'

'Oww!' She pulled a horrified face, but he could see she was looking forward to it, relishing the fuss she could make. 'When you're a doctor, you can fix all my blisters.'

'Yeah.'

She put the shoes back on. 'Will you have to go away to be a doctor?'

'I suppose so. After my A-levels. I'll have to go to university, and then I'll have to go to a hospital to practise all the doctor stuff. Y'know. Fixing blisters. Chopping people into little bits!'

'Eeee!'

He let her sink her head on to his shoulder. 'What do you want to be, Becca?'

'I want to be a teacher. Like Miss Rose.'

For a moment, he was dressed in a white coat, dressing some minor wound on Miss Rose's hand. Better still, a cracked rib. '*I'm afraid you'll have to take your top off, Miss Rose.*' '*Call me Lisa . . . David!*'

He looked down at his hands. They'd have to change. He couldn't see this pair delving into a red, live abdomen, or drawing out a new baby. Writing a prescription across a desk from Miss Rose, or an old lady, or someone like his father. Perhaps the only way would really be to grow new ones, peeling out of his skin, taking off the old hands like rubber gloves. But, even now, he felt different to who he'd been that morning.

He stretched, a real stretch, and his sister's head slid down his chest. She was asleep. Awkwardly, he reached into his pocket for the sugar Mona Lisas. One was cracked, so he ate that, keeping the whole one for Miss Rose. After a while he ate the whole one too. He licked the sugar from his lips, tasting it like a wasp, and, behind the sweetness, there was the lingering tang of French cologne.

iii. Quiet

YOU CAN SCARE YOURSELF if you want to. Watch airport-disaster films the week before you fly, then ask for a window seat and sit goggling at the wings. Trace the lines where the wires must be, see the frail structure buffeting in the wind. Or you can take a drink, that sock to the jaw, and sleep the journey through. They tell you to drink water. The air in the cabin dries you out, and the pressure does something; it pushes the alcohol into your bloodstream, drives it like traffic through your veins. Well, that will do me fine. When the stewardesses make their first solicitous trip up the aisle, I will ask for doubles and tell them not to wake me for the meal. Play the dozy old lady and slip under the radar of their attention. I'm not one of those fools who has to strike up a relationship with them. It's a hard living, being friendly, harder than any amount of ditch digging or truck driving, which is why they give it to these wee girls. So. A quick smile, with a flash of eye contact, to show that I'm courteous but not eager and will be no trouble to them. *Yes,* I will tell them, *I'm sure about the meal. Really.*

When I first started visiting Moira, I used to read on the plane. I bought the books that you're supposed to. Big doorstoppers with the author's name in foily capitals. They tired me out; carrying them and reading them, fighting to hold the covers open, like trying to undo a hedgehog. But then I found a little book about Body Language in the business section of the airport bookshop. Now I read people instead.

I don't see fidgeting any more; I see Displacement Gestures

and Auto Contact. The woman playing with her seat belt wants to jump up and run screaming down the aisle. The businessman touching his mouth, smoothing his hair, is just a big baby on the scary plane, reminding himself of his mammy. Eighty per cent of people do things like that on a transatlantic flight, and those who don't are superior, or peculiar, or me. Or stewardesses. *They* reassure folk with their Overkill Smiles, and squeeze down the aisle with their gaze averted, their hands raised, in an innocent, sexless brushing of bodies.

I take my seat quickly and lay out my Territorial Markers. Belongings are good, but clothes are best. Clothes are personal, almost like skin. I put my coat over the back of my seat to ward folk off my head; it's a Taboo Zone, the head, restricted to lovers and parents and Head Professionals, like doctors and hairdressers. Then I fold my arms (The Body Cross) and try to look as if I have been here for years. Expressionless. An Easter Island statue woman, going on a plane.

A young girl comes counting up the aisle:

'Thirty-one, thirty-two, here we are!'

She has patty little hands, and she runs her fingers over the seat, the head rest, making them her own. Just like a dog cocking its leg, the book said. Her boyfriend – husband – (*new* husband, she wears a pair of shiny rings) – follows on with their bags. He's exaggeratedly cool, acting bored, but he holds the bags protectively over his groin area. Men, eh? He passes the bags to the girl, and she reaches up to put them in the locker. It would have been her who packed both their cases, rolling the boy's socks into buns and fattening his shoes with them. He's more the sitting-on-the-cases-to-close-them type. That's not the book, that's just me.

The girl's sweater rides up, exposing an inch of back, soft skin with the vertebrae showing like abacus beads. The boy makes a sudden lunge, a tickling attack, and she squeaks and skips, and bangs her head.

'Oww! Stop it, Jamie!'

Don't worry! He's only displacing his Flight or Fight Response.

'I don't know why they call them *overhead* lockers!' he says, indignant, like it was him who banged his head. He is tall, and tall men are always saying things like that to remind you of it. He'll complain about the leg room soon.

The girl stands back – 'There!' – and he steps in to do his Tall Job; slams the locker door, too hard, so it bounces out of its catch and he has to slam it again. The sort of person who doesn't perceive noise; or who needs to hear himself, to know he's alive. The girl catches my eye and winces apologetically:

'Sorry!'

I smile her an *okay*!

The boy drops himself into the window seat and squirms about, his leather jacket squeaking. 'Not much leg room!'

'D'you want the aisle seat, then, Jamie?'

'Nah. Thanks.' The window seat is prime; he wants it. But he sits there looking like a cat in a pram, trapped and miserable.

The girl pokes her fingers into the rude-looking air vents, presses the Stewardess Call button by mistake – 'Oops!' – but no-one comes. Nothing is turned on yet. I hope she calms down soon. No wonder she's thin, gyrating about like bacon on a hot griddle.

She peeks over the boy's shoulder at the baggage handlers outside.

'God, look how they're throwing them around! Someone's brought a cardboard box instead of a case . . . isn't that weird? Oops! There it goes!'

'Probably someone's cat. Probably going to spend the whole journey upside-down.'

I recognise something angry in his voice, a hostility to his teasing. It's the girl; her talking irritates him. She's doing it because she's nervous. It reminds him that he's nervous too.

He puts on a child's falsetto: ' "Mummy, why is Puss so cold and still?" '

'*Don't*, Jamie!' The girl mock-punches him. 'Oh, that's it! They're closing the passenger door. Hurry up, baggage men!' She makes whooshing gestures with her hands to speed them on. The boy shakes his head.

* * *

The cold daylight from the doorway shuts off and I feel the effect straight away; the air stuffed into my ears. I hold my nose like a diver, shake my head. The cabin pressure seems to thicken the sound and push it straight into your brain via the nostrils. The engine's pick-up buzzes in my joints, my jaw. Even now, people are still fussing, remembering things that they might want from their lockers. Familiar objects to make them feel safe. Easier if the airlines were just to hand out teddy bears. The stewardesses sweep down the aisles and press the passengers like pegs into their seats. At the front of the plane, they turn on their smart heels and start doing their safety dance. I roll up my maggoty yellow ear plugs and poke them into place, make up my own commentary: *This is how to occupy yourself as we plunge towards the sea. The fighting will break out at the doors here – here – and here.* Big smile. *We are all fish food.*

I close my eyes.

When I open them again, the seat-belt light is off, and the stewardesses are clanking their cabaret of drinks at the front of the plane. A wave of talk comes up the aisle: people discussing the important matter of what they're going to have. God forbid they should sit staring glumly at a Malibu for twenty minutes when they wanted a Tia Maria.

'Here come the trolley dollies,' says the boy. 'Would you fancy that job, Becca?'

'No thanks! I've already done my share of waitressing. That's all it is, isn't it? A glorified waitress.'

'You've got to be really pretty.'

'Thanks!'

'And there's a height requirement.' He flexes at the stewardess in a lanky stretch. Ritual Display. The girl smooths back a lock of his hair. Re-establishing the Pair Bond.

A kid starts squawking a few rows ahead, something in French, and for a second I think it's one of Moira's. The last time that I visited, the older boy did a project on me, like I was an artefact. He showed it to me, but he didn't say it was in French, and, for a moment, I thought I'd had a stroke; the page of words looked like words should, but wouldn't give up their meaning. It hadn't occurred to him that I wouldn't be bilingual. He talked me through it when he realised, pointed out words:

'*Grand-mère.* That's you, Grandma.' *Grenmah.*

'French school?' I asked Moira later.

'They like immigrants to send their kids there in Quebec. Besides, we want to integrate.'

Now that I'm *on my own* (happily married themselves, they say it like it's an illness), they want me to come out and integrate with them. I'm not sure. They don't have pensioners in Canada, they have Seniors instead. Vigorous old buggers who won't leave you alone, who have to recruit you like Moonies into their time-filling classes – *klehsis.* They have Exercise Klehsis and Dence Klehsis. I could take French Klehsis if I wanted to. Moira showed me a brochure.

'Look – Jewish Cookery classes. You won't have that at home.'

Right enough.

The stewardess is uneasy about letting me go without food.

'Have some peanuts, at least!' Holding them up to her chest, encouraging, like a KP girl pinned up over a bar.

'No! *Thank* you!' This is definitely going against the book. Eating together is friendly. Refusing food is refusing to bond with the group. Everyone else will do the Food Stare, hunting the meal with their eyes until it reaches their laps. But I've tasted those meals and, at my age, it's a long way to the toilets. It could be anything, coated in that red-tasting stew. And the bread rolls! I don't know if they're buns or ballast, if they're only there to weigh the tray down. You may as well eat a grenade. So I fight the urge to be amenable, keep my hands in my lap until she gives up and lets me have a fistful of brandy miniatures and a plastic cup. But she doesn't like it.

The boy can't decide between whisky and beer.

'You can have both!'

'Great!'

Big smile. Everyone is smiling at each other, the stewardess widening her crimson grin: *you see, some people know how to behave*!

'Will you have the steak or the chicken?'

They both want the steak.

'You should have the chicken, Becca. To try it. We shouldn't both have the same thing.' Perhaps he thinks the stewardess will offer them both of the meals as well.

'Steak,' says the girl.

'Sure?'

'Yes, thanks.'

After a while, she says:

'I'll have what I want.'

The boy raises his eyebrows. 'Oo-ooh!' Mocking her. She turns her face away and looks at a stain on the floor with fierce concentration. I'll bet she's a champion sulker. When her gaze finally breaks, I'm ready to catch her eye, and I wink at her, making her grin. She seems to consider it, then winks back. I lean slightly towards her so that, once we've exchanged a few words, I can lean back to signify that the conversation is over.

'Are you on honeymoon?'

She smiles.

'No, we're going to live in Montreal. We're emigrating! My husband –' a blush – 'My husband has got a job out there. With Bell. You know? The telephones.'

I lean forward to smile at him past the girl's shoulder, but he draws back: shy, or arrogant, or a bit of both.

'Lovely!' I say. 'My daughter lives in Montreal.'

But the girl is too young to think of asking about her. 'I'm hoping to teach out there,' she says. 'English. I know I'll have to read up on some of the Canadian authors, but I'm looking forward to that.'

'Lovely!' I nod. But I remember the phone call from Moira in her first week in Quebec. When she'd been to the employment offices and come back 'as mad as hell'.

'Well . . .' I say, 'You know you'll have to learn French, don't you? You can't teach there without it.'

The girl gapes.

'Oh! Oh no! I thought, with English . . . oh!' She turns to the boy. 'Did you hear that? I'll have to learn French!'

'So? Learn French!'

She doubles her fists, strikes them on her knees.

'We know nothing!' she says bitterly. 'We're going out there and we know nothing!'

'I'm sorry if I upset you, dear . . .'

'No, it's best to know.' But she sweeps her bag up and heads for the toilets. The boy looks across, but says nothing. He sips his beer and turns his face to the window.

Fine. Me and my big mouth. I put my ear plugs back in and tilt the seat so I can sleep.

I wake once. The girl is back, reading a book. Margaret Atwood: a thick compilation, the spine arched over her knees. The boy is dozing, his arm slung across her shoulder.

I close my eyes again.

This is my favourite part of the journey, when everyone has settled down; far enough along to start digging out their magazines and crosswords, their personal stereos. I know how to ward off the chatterers: crossed arms, the nod and jerk of falling asleep. If they persist, I feign deafness, or a stammer. Three sentences are usually their limit then. If they're very insistent, I pretend to feel sick.

I should have bought that book years ago. There's a chapter on International Insults. I could have communicated in gestures when Dougie was going through one of his silent phases.

I could have pointed to the bunched fingers of my left hand:

Dougie, you are the son of a whore. (Saudi Arabia.)

I could have done the beard stroke:

Dougie, you are boring. (Most of Europe.)

Or I could have done the gypsy symbol for:

You are a pansy!

For that, you squeeze your hand around an imaginary, soft object. Mind you, I think Dougie could have interpreted that one himself.

'Can you not be quiet?' he would say. 'I've got things to think about. I don't have your mania for *small talk.*'

Sniffy bugger. Didn't have any big talk either.

When I left, I thought of writing him a letter with all the things that I thought of him, leaving him the information as other women leave dinners in the oven. But in the end, I just put a note on the kitchen table. Not on paper – *on* the kitchen table, in marker pen. Big letters, like a shout:

QUIET NOW, EH?

And after that, I found that I didn't need to talk so much. It had been him all along; I had been trying to fill his vacuum.

A banging at my seat wakes me up. Sometimes you get a kicker behind you, or someone for whom putting the seat tray up is a Mensa test. The only thing then is to get round there and invade their Personal Space; spit when you talk, make it worse for them than for you. But it's the stewardess. She's hitting the trolley against my seat; revenge, no doubt, for being un-cooperative. I turn over, clench my eyes, try to grab at the sleep again, to pull it over me like a warm blanket . . . but she keeps at it, bang bang bang, until I have to sit up. This is too much.

'Listen, you lipsticked bitch . . .'

My own voice, loud in my head. I still have the ear plugs in. Sounds woof and roar around me, muffled, nightmarish; shouting and shrieks. The plane is in uproar, the stewardess frantic, pulling at the trolley; she skews it left and right, then abandons it and runs off down the aisle. People are on their feet, on their seats, jumping and yelling. I pull out the ear plugs, and the noise slams in like a film soundtrack, like a sonic boom.

'What is it?' At the top of my voice, but no-one answers. 'What's happening? Is it a crash?' And I think suddenly of my suitcase, of the presents in the hold and what a waste they'll be now. Moira's kids. It suddenly becomes very important to remember their birthdays, and I can't even remember their names.

Something tumbles past my feet, small and brown, and I register it as a blown leaf, which can't be right. It stops under the seat in front of me, and I see it properly now, buzzing with clarity, in astonishing 3D. Dark eyes and whiskers, a curled tail. A mouse. A field mouse. It must have come in off the airfield.

'Don't worry!' I say. I'm saying it to myself. 'It's just a little mouse.'

But you don't just *see* a mouse. Mice carry mouse-ideas, like viruses: of women on chairs and wedges of cheese, of a spill of rice in the cupboard and bite-sized holes in the packet, and running up clocks (*why?*). Birds fly into plane engines – can mice do that? If I look out of the window, will I see slices of mice spraying from the chopping engine, and hear a splutter and a squeak before we drop into the sea? The kids, Moira's kids, singing: M-I-C-K-E-Y, M-O-U-S-E! Disney addicts, the pair of them. Bernard and Louis, that's what they're called. What a stupid pair of names! And there's the mouse, still in front of me, and I don't know if I said all that aloud.

The trolley slides aside and the girl across the aisle is looking at me, her face flushed.

'Is it there?'

'It's by my feet.'

We're almost whispering, but we hear each other clearly, in a bubble of understanding. She holds up her handbag. It's empty, she has tipped it out; lipstick and plasters and her purse, like a stain on the seat.

'They like the dark,' she says, nodding at the bag. 'I'll try to catch it in here.'

I lean back for her to move in beside me.

'There it is! Oh, it's so frightened!'

We look at the mouse. It's trembling, its own throbbing heart giving it away. I keep my feet still as the girl comes in closer, crouching, moving imperceptibly. The mouse makes a small shiver, a tiny shift in the focus of its attention. It can't fail to be aware of the bag now. It seems to be wondering if it would be so bad, after all, to creep inside. I think of *Tom and Jerry* cartoons, the mouse running into the cat's open mouth, making a shape in its tail. Are they aware of traps? Its nose twitches, reading the smells.

A shadow, and the tang of leather.

The boy's foot stamps down between us.

The mouse disappears, its place taken by the boy's boot, and for a moment I think he's crushed it and that he will peel it off his foot – flat, with cleat marks in its body. But then it's out again, down the aisle, under the trolley, with the boy leaping after it, trampling at it with his thick soles. I'm drawn into the mouse's small scale, how it must be: like rocks falling around you, like planes dropping out of the sky. The boy whoops as he chases it, blundering through the rows of seats.

One of the pilots emerges at the front of the plane. He sweeps off his hat, stoops, looking ridiculously gallant. He scrabbles, scoops, and a cheer goes up.

'Got it!'

The passengers applaud. Now everyone is a mouse expert:

'It must have been attracted by the smell of the food.'

'That's right!'

They start going back to their seats, and the stewardesses reappear, sheepish at their loss of control. They start to serve more drinks, calming down the passengers and themselves.

The boy comes back up the aisle, looking sullen.

'I almost had it!'

The girl stares at him.

'What?' he says, frowning, confused at the lack of a hero's welcome. Then his face slides into realisation. 'Oh. Aw, c'mon Becca; they're going to kill it anyway.'

The girl shakes her head.

'They are, they'll have to. It's a live animal. Aw, don't be silly . . .'

The Victorians perfected the art of The Cut. We still say that we 'cut someone dead'. The point is that, having seen someone, having *shown* that you've seen them, you pretend that they don't exist. The ultimate insult. In our democratic times, it takes a lot of control.

The girl won't speak, and now he's angry at her silence. He tries to cajole her for a while, then he swears and turns away, ostentatiously ignoring her, trying to outdo her. She picks up her book and sits, not reading, but punishing the pages, turning them too fast. They'll speak again as the end of the journey gets closer. She'll have his tickets and he'll have her passport, and they'll pitch themselves together against the strangeness of the new country. But it'll be quiet enough for now.

iv. Fruit and Flowers

'IT'S LIKE A PARTY!'

It's the trodden crisps and dished pickles, the vinegared salmon sandwiches with dry bread curling like fish tails. The salmon has whiskery bones in, spiked with slivers of paper, trapped by the tin opener and missed in the mashing.

'The thing is', says my brother, 'it *is* a party. But I know what you mean; it's like a *kids'* party.'

Both our birthdays fall in the summer, so the elements are right. We remember this: street noises through the open window, passing cars and the round thump of a football. The sounds reach in on the late afternoon warmth, bright sparks in the cigarette-voiced indoor hum. There are so many relatives packed into the living room that no-one misses you if you cut out to stand alone on the lawn, dressy heels sinking in the earth and the strangeness of Aunty Bella's best crystal in your hand. But now I am side-saddle on the shiny arm of the sofa, and my brother stands behind me like a standard lamp.

'All we need now is balloons,' he says. 'Can you get funeral balloons?'

'Black balloons! With skulls on.'

'With RIP.'

'And death-rattle blowers. And a badge: *I am dead.*'

'We could play Spin the Bottle; find out who's going to be next.'

'Ugh! Too much, sick bag! You'll be upsetting Aunty Ann.' I

look down at her wispy lilac head, with the baby skull showing through the hair. She is on the sofa beside me, shaking a cup violently in its saucer.

'She can't hear me.'

'Yes she can,' says Aunty Ann, without turning round. 'David's a wicked boy. Only Becca loves her Aunty Ann.'

I stroke her shoulder.

'Only Becca would go and put a drop of brandy in her aunty's tea . . .' She trembles the cup in my direction. My brother slides down on to the floor at her feet and starts chatting her up, crooning softly.

I take the cup to the row of optics on the wall: a mini-pub, with a boat-shaped bar underneath. I work out how to pour a measure by pressing with my fingers, and the vacuum-smell of brandy rises in the steamy tea, burning the air.

Gramps had a tea caddy on his kitchen wall, with a button that measured out the tea. David hoisted me up, but we still couldn't reach it.

'We'll have to get a chair,' he said. We were dragging the chair over when Gramps came back from the toilet and caught us.

'*Tea leaves*', he said, 'is Cockney rhyming slang for *thieves*!'

But when he saw us blush, he was sorry.

'Go on then, you.'

He stood us under the caddy and pressed the button, solemnly dispensing the tea leaves over us.

'It's raining!' he cried.

I pretended I was a lady taking a shower. Afterwards, the three of us danced in the garden to shake off the tea before our parents came back to take us home. When they arrived, we looked at each other and laughed and didn't tell them about it, and, that night, there was tea in my vest.

Taking the tea back, I pass my father. He is sitting with the men, a greying boy in a black suit. They are choosing a Welsh First Fifteen, and, later, he may be allowed to suggest a sub. I try to catch his eye, but he is lost in thought. The men talk around him and Aunty Bella's baggy spaniel snuffles like a manatee at the plate on his lap, licking up the remains of a ham sandwich. It can't believe its luck. He turns its soft ears over in his hands and holds them gently, like gloves.

'Aunty Ann?'

'Ah! Becca's a good girl! Aunty Ann is going to leave all her lovely jewels to Becca.'

Jealous cousins turn their heads; but I know that Aunty Ann's lovely jewels are just a magpie box of coloured beads and diamanté.

My brother stands up in his tall suit, and we watch Aunty Ann sucking her tea.

'Gramps' sister!' he says quietly. 'Gramps' *little* sister!'

'Imagine! Aunty Ann as a little girl! Wearing high-button boots and . . . and climbing a tree!'

He closes his eyes.

'No good. I can only see her like she is now. Like she is now up a tree, mind. Look.' He pretends to pluck the image from his forehead, cupping it like an egg and flattening it on to my brow. I close my eyes.

'Shocking! What legs!' I open my eyes again. 'Do you think they see themselves as old?'

'Nah. They probably see the young face. Remember it. Old Annie's a devilish flirt.'

'Yeah. Probably surprised at how old their siblings are. Tell you what, though, I can imagine Gramps as a kid.'

'Big ears!' we say together.

'Can't you see *him* up a tree, Dave!'

'He got on the shed once, remember? Couldn't get down for ages. Like a bloody cat.'

'Longest game of hide-and-seek I've ever had!'

'We should've told the vicar. He could have mentioned it at the service. Would have gone down well with this lot.'

He gestures around at Gramps' remaining brothers and sisters. Of the original thirteen, only four are left. They have come from around the country for the funeral, but they don't seem to want to be together. Annie is curled and warming around her brandy, and gnomish Ned stands at the table, tucking cakes into his pockets. His big little brother Jack, a giant of an ex-miner with missing fingers, sits next to my father, saying nothing but hacking into the conversation with his anthracite laugh. Flossie, in Sunday black but with a hat for Easter, where birds might comfortably nest and peck at the painted cherries, is showing round a picture of her wedding. She brings the photograph to David and me.

'Look! Wasn't I beautiful? See my hair! I used to brush it a hundred times before I went to bed.'

'And then she would kick Annie all night,' says Aunty Ann.

'Annie was always jealous of my hair.'

'She should have had it cut off. It drained the strength from her brains.' Aunty Ann takes a sly peek at the photograph, then looks closer. 'Flossie's a fool! That's Annie's wedding!'

Flossie's face falls under the gauzy hat.

'No!'

'That photograph belongs to Annie! Give it back!'

They cheep at each other like birds until Aunty Bella intervenes. Bella has recently had a cataract removed. She has already made David look at her eye in a whispering consultation in the bathroom, and she wears a patch over it; but I can see from Annie and Flossie's faces that they have forgotten this. She takes the photo from them.

'Solomon's Judgement,' she says sternly, though Flossie is her mother.

'Not fair!' cries Flossie, and she slaps Annie, a quick dab on the shoulder, and scuttles away.

David tells me: 'You'll be like that one day.'

'*You* will!'

'*You* will!'

'Here, kids,' says Bella, turning her head sideways to look at the photograph, 'that's your Gramps as a young man.'

We crowd in to look. He's standing at the back with his hat on. His grin is blurred, but we know the eyes, the ears sticking out from his silly, handsome face. The hat makes him look like a spiv;

nothing to do with the wedding party, just someone who turned up on the off-chance of selling some hot watches.

'That hat was still in his wardrobe,' says Aunty Bella.

Of course it was. We recognise it.

'You look like gangsters!' said Gramps, knotting the tie around my neck. 'Now, where did I put my guns? Hmm.'

My brother looked at him anxiously under the brim of the hat. He had begun to wonder recently whether Gramps was babysitting us, or vice versa.

'No, I can't remember. We'll have to use alternative weapons.'

I got a walking stick and David got an umbrella. Gramps showed us how to carry them, crooked over our forearms, ready to aim and fire.

'But don't shoot unless you have to. If we do this right, no-one will get hurt. You dirty rats!' he added.

We looked left, right, left on the deserted Saturday road, and crossed to the corner shop.

'Hello Joe!' Mrs Evans was marzipaned in a wide, yellow pinny; she rolled around behind the counter like a gob stopper, and laughed with cherry lips. 'Lemon drops, is it?'

'The dame's wise to us,' whispered Gramps. 'Keep me covered; I'll do the talking.'

Trembling, we aimed at Mrs Evans as she weighed the sweets into a paper bag and twisted it into a snout.

'Anything else?'

'Better have two sherbet dabs for the children. Can you put it on the slate?' To us he whispered: 'See how I didn't use your names?'

'Right you are.' Mrs Evans turned for the sherbet dabs, and Gramps reached quickly over the counter and undid the strings of her apron. She looked down at the sudden flap of cloth and giggled.

'Oh, Joe! You *are* a boy!'

Gramps pocketed the sweets. 'Thanks, doll-face! Right, gang, let's blow this joint!'

Safe in the kitchen, we choked gratefully on our sherbert while Gramps sucked on two lemon drops at once.

'You observed that I didn't pay?' he mumbled.

We nodded.

'That's the thing, you see. If you run a campaign of intimidation successfully, you hardly ever have to shoot anyone.'

And he pulled the hat over David's eyes.

'Have you still got the hat, Aunty Bella?'

She skews her head to look at me. 'It's upstairs. I was going to give it to the jumble. Why? Do you want it?'

'Please!'

We hear her swearing and slipping on the stairs.

'Are you watching the time?' asks David. I am catching a flight home later and he's running me to the airport.

'Right enough. I suppose I'd better go and say goodbye.'

My father looks like he's forgotten that I was going.

'I'll be back soon,' I tell him. 'I'll bring Jamie next time.'

'Is Jamie not here, then?' He's bewildered, suffering from grief and an overdose of relatives. I hug him until he says *Oof!*, and get lipstick on his funeral suit. Jack gives me his strange, four-fingered squeeze, and Ned, with a sandwich in each hand, hugs me at arm's length, worried that I will squash his cakes.

In the kitchen, we interrupt a production line of food. My female relatives, smart in navy and black, have aprons and dishcloths swagged around their waists. They jostle each other with their elbows, spreading butter and gossip, voices raised in a domestic shanty:

'Is there a bread knife?'

'Here, love.'

'Thanks, love!'

I wave at my mother over the sea of hairdos. She looks small and lost in this crew of mothers. They're all uneasy in the territory of someone else's kitchen, and this elaborate activity is their way of coping, of bonding.

My mother fights her way through to me.

'Going already?'

But she would say this whatever time I left. She is tiny and sweet-smelling in my arms, her face powdered and downy like a forlorn little peach.

Aunty Bella, the pirate queen, bounces in off the kitchen doorpost, carrying the hat.

'Here it is!'

'Is that Joe's?'

'It's Joe's hat!'

David perches it on his head, and they all exclaim:

'He's the living spit!'

'That's Joe to the life!'

He clowns in it, holding his ears out, kissing the women. Reaching behind my mother, he undoes her apron.

'Ooh, you bugger!'

She takes the apron off and wipes her hands in it. The women take off their aprons too, in some instinctive farewell etiquette, and pass me along in a chain of embraces. I retrieve my coat, and kiss and hug my way out, stopping to pet Aunty Ann in her chair.

In the front garden, Aunty Flossie is picking a bunch of flowers; her hat is already full of them, and she has tucked one, ticket-style, under the windscreen wiper of David's car, obscuring the 'Doctor on Call' sign. As we drive away, she whirls the bouquet around her head in salute.

These are visiting streets, the route we used to come to see Aunty Bella as children. It feels odd and vaguely naughty to be sitting in the front of the car, with David driving. We cross the hump-backed bridge where our father used to accelerate to make us say *Whoo*! David does it now, and I coo obediently. He still has the hat on.

As the corner shop comes into view, he slows the car.

'What d'you think, Becca? Got time to stop?'

Gramps' front door.

'Just a minute then.'

There is already an estate agent's sign on the lawn, and the net curtains have been taken down. We look through the window, into the empty room where Gramps had his bed for the last two years; where, only a few days ago, he went to sleep and didn't wake up.

'You must have seen quite a few bodies, Dave.'

'Hmm.'

'Do you see them as people any more? Or are they just . . . I don't know. Just so much meat?'

'No.' He speaks to my reflection in the window. 'You have to stay aware of it. The humanity. You have to keep the *wonder*.'

He shakes himself and looks about.

'Come on. Round the side.'

We don't have a key, but David gives me a leg up over the side wall into the back garden, throwing the hat over before jumping after me.

'If anyone comes, we'll say we're thinking of buying.'

There are cobwebs over the toilet at the end of the garden, and a tatter of Izal paper on the roll. The oil lamp in the corner, which used to stop the water freezing in the winter, is cold.

Outside, I point out the stone with *Timmy* scratched on it, the name of Gramps' old dog. David picks a flower and places it on the grave.

'This is becoming a habit!' he says, trying to laugh.

In the greenhouse, Gramps' tomato plants press their fingery leaves, their red cheeks, against the glass. Inside, it is warm and humid, the heavy, green smell giving a salad taste to the air.

'Look; these are spoiling.' I pluck an over-ripe fruit from its vine. It comes easily, dropping its fat weight into my hand. The skin splits, yielding juice into the lines of my palm.

Gramps spent whole summers here, while we played on the lawn with props that he had dug out from the shed. He had a child's imagination, and it was enough for him to find a blackbird's feather on the path to set him making a clothes-horse teepee, where we could be Red Indians all afternoon. We would tie him to the deck chair while he slept, or pretend he was captive in the greenhouse, a prisoner who sang while he tended his plants. He grew far too many tomatoes for himself, although he would eat dishes of them, sprinkled with sugar.

'Sugar, Gramps!'

'It's the only way. Lloyd George ate his tomatoes like this.'

But it was his pleasure to heap them into bags, passing them over the wall to the neighbours, giving us basketfuls to take home with us, and refusing thanks.

'Pity to waste them!'

'Pity to waste them,' says David. 'We should pick a few. We could put them in the hat.'

But before he can take it off, I have aimed and hit him on the back of the head with the tomato, knocking the hat over his eyes.

'God!' He turns round. 'For a minute, I thought it was him!' He stoops for the tomato and bowls it back at me. I pull more ammo from the plant, and then we are launched on a full-scale tomato fight, laughing and crying at the same time, our whoops and yells echoing around the greenhouse, and the thud of fruit on the glass.

We are covered in the ripe flesh. David's suit is spattered with tomato gore; I have seeds and jelly smeared on my clothes, my hair. I will have to fly back on the plane like this.

I wipe my hands on my skirt.

'Right, gang! Let's blow this joint!'

v. Touch and Go

THE STEWARD HAD GIVEN me an activity book, but it was for *little* kids. Barney the Dinosaur.

'An activity book to keep you still!' said my mother. When she wasn't looking, I drew a pair of ladies' bosoms on all the pictures of Barney, big W's with two little dots hanging like earrings off the bottom. The fat girl who was Barney's friend was smiling up at his bosoms now. I would deal with her later.

The man from the end seat came back and sat next to my mother, happy and noisy and making a fuss. He'd been talking non-stop since the plane took off. He was from Norway; but not just now. Just now he was back from the toilet. He seemed very pleased with himself about it.

'I am in oil,' he told my mother. I stopped crayoning and looked at him. He nodded at her as if he wanted her to approve of something, and his thick glasses made his eyes bobble up and down. His hair was certainly slicked back with something, but he wasn't in oil.

'I travel everywhere, but mostly to America. I have travelled in all of America, and England, like Aberdeen.'

'In oil,' said my mother.

'In oil,' he agreed, and she blew her nose in her serviette, a booger snort, like you do in school to hide that you're laughing. Imagine my mother knowing that.

I drew a round face and gave it big glasses, and eyes that filled the lenses, like eyeballs with frames that you could take right off your face. I wanted yellow for the man's hair, but my mother had packed the wrong crayons and I had to use orange.

'I think your small boy is drawing me,' said the oil man.

'He's a girl,' said my mother. '*She's* a girl. It's the hat.'

She pulled my baseball cap off to show him my hair, and stroked my head. There was a cold feeling of hat where it had been. I grabbed it off her and put it on again, but I could still feel the touch of her hand.

I opened the carrier bag to see what else she had brought. It was a clothes bag, thick and shiny, bits of it surprising me by going into sudden, sharp folds, leaving white drag marks in my skin. I put my face to it and my breath raised hot plastic smells, and the reek of pencil shavings. The bag had been in the car when she picked me up from school.

'Mom?'

She never came to meet me. I always walked home with Avra through Westmount Park, stopping at the water fountain in the summer, sliding on the ice in winter. I thought maybe it was because of the snow. The sky had been red with it all morning and, after lunch, it started to fall, making the afternoon dark, covering the lines on the school tennis courts. My mother didn't even have snow chains on the car. And she didn't have gloves, her fingers were white, pink at the tips. She'd been waiting for me.

'Where are we going? Are we going home? Can Avra come round?'

'Get in the car.'

'Mom?'

'And do your coat up. Quickly!'

I climbed in and buckled up. 'Mom? Uh-oh, it's not the dentist, is it?'

She turned the car in a wide, slithery circle in the street. A taxi driver hooted at her, and she gave him the finger.

'Mo-om!'

'We're going on a trip. That'll be nice, won't it?'

'Where's Dad?'

'We're going to see Nana and Grampa and Uncle David.'

'We're going on a *plane*?'

'Yup.'

'Where's Dad? Is he at the aéroport?'

'Airport. Your father's not coming.'

I thought about this.

'Mom, you're driving really fast . . .'

Some of the pencils had broken, their points rolling like coloured gems in the bottom of the bag. One with a point had pricked its way through the plastic, like it was showing off to the broken ones. There was no eraser. My mother had just chucked these things in. There was my book about horses, which was good, but a stupid counting book too, and my mother's diary.

'That's private!' she said when she saw it, and took it off me.

'I wasn't reading it!' I looked in the bag again. 'There's no more paper. Mom, I want to draw!'

'Here.' She tore some blank pages from the diary. They had *Notes* printed at the top, and grey lines. I started to design a house, putting vertical lines on the horizontal grey to make bricks.

The steward came round offering drinks. He spoke like a girl.

'I would like champagne,' said the oil man.

'Champagne! Cool!'

'You can have juice!' said my mother.

The steward smiled at me with all his teeth. 'We have apple or orange, sir!'

I took my hat off and his teeth disappeared.

'*Cer*tainly do!' he added lamely, trying to disguise it.

'Apple.' I said.

'This lady will also have champagne,' said the oil man about my mother.

'Ooh, I don't know . . .'

'But yes! It is too lonely to drink champagne on yourself. We will think of a thing to celebrate. Do you have a thing to celebrate?'

'Well . . .' My mother balled her hands into a fist, then threw them open. 'Why not? It's not every day we travel Club Class!'

* * *

We had been bumped up to Club Class as late arrivals. My mother parked the car like a cop show, squealing sideways to a halt.

'Run! Run!'

The weight of the suitcase made her look like she was skipping, like Maria in *The Sound of Music*. They'd put it on in the pre-Christmas schedule. It sucked.

'We can get a cart, Mom.'

'No time!'

The snow was wet here, run down into grey slush by the cars and the shuttle buses. People looked at us as we ran along the concourse, past the shops selling stuffed mooses and beavers and cans of maple syrup. My mother puffed her name to the clerk at the Air Canada desk.

'Rebecca Blake. I called earlier.'

'You just made it,' said the clerk. 'Touch and go, eh!' After she'd checked our bags and given us our tickets, telling us that we'd been bumped up, she yelled after us: 'Have a good trip now!'

The oil man was having a good trip. He ordered more champagne, tried to pour another glass for my mother, but she shook her head, laughing.

'I'd better pace myself! Can't turn up rolling. Drunk,' she explained. 'Drunk in charge of a child,' she added, nodding at me. 'What sort of mother would I be?'

The oil man looked at her seriously. 'But no! My dear mother gets shit-faced every time she is in an aeroplane!'

My mother choked. 'Well, *my* dear mother would have a fit if I turned up, er, tipsy! No, really –' He tried to pour her a glass, and she put her hand over it to stop him.

She wasn't wearing her wedding band. I hadn't noticed in the car. There was a mark like a burn on her ring finger, the skin shining and white.

I knew about burns. My mother was clumsy in the kitchen, always hurrying to have the meal ready when my father got home. I would hear her swearing under her breath while I did my school assignments at the breakfast bar. If my father was away, I could have Avra round after school, perhaps even have a sleep over. But my father didn't like the house 'full of kids'. One time he came home early, and Avra said that my mother almost broke her arm trying to get her coat on.

'Oh, Jamie!' said my mother. 'Avra was just going!'

Avra said 'Hi, Jamie!' She couldn't learn to call parents *Mr* and *Mrs.* She called my mother 'Becca', like her mother did. My father went like a bottle of Coke, all shaken up with the lid still on. After Avra left, the lid came off. I went up to my room and closed the window so that people outside wouldn't hear the fighting. I'd seen my mother do that. When I went down again, we had to have Pizza Dino because my mother had dropped the pan with the dinner in it. She'd burnt her arm, there was a blister the size of a hockey ball.

What you do with burns is, you run a sink of cold water and hold the burn under, no matter how much it hurts. You hold it under until you can't stand it any more.

The oil man fell asleep. His eyelashes looked enormous through the glasses: two spiders that had crawled on to his face, but blond, like the spiders you find in the basement that never see the sun. It gave me an idea for Barney's fat friend. On every page, I covered her with spiders, put webs over her mouth. I branched out into beetles and monster wasps. She cried squirting, clown tears as the wasps stung her arms, her face, her fat butt.

My mother read her diary. She read it like a book, laughing at some bits, gasping and frowning at others. Now and then she said to me:

'Remember? Remember we went to *La Ronde* and there was lightning?' Or 'Remember we went to the sugar shack? And all those Hell's Angels were line-dancing?'

As she read each page, she tore it out and stuffed it into the magazine rack. When she had ripped out all the written days, she gave me what was left. Just a few weeks, the weeks before Christmas, and three pages into the New Year, to make up the space.

'You can have that,' she said. 'You can do what you want with that.'

I made a fleet of tiny planes from the pages, and we threw them, flew them at each other. My mother got the giggles, shushed me.

'Shh!'

'Who's giggling? Hey! Who's giggling, Mom?' I tickled her under the arms.

'Don't! You'll wake the man!'

'He's *too* friendly!'

'Yeah!' She preened, laughing. 'I think I've clicked there!'

'It's because you took your wedding band off,' I said, and she stopped laughing. She sat up in the seat, straight and serious, and stroked my forehead.

'Sweetie . . .'

'Uh huh?'

'When we visited Nana and Grampa last time, well, you liked it, didn't you?'

'I guess so. I don't remember much. I was young then.'

'You were, weren't you! Not all grown up like you are now!'

'You're kidding me,' I said. 'Stop kidding me.'

'You're right. I'm sorry.' She looked at me, a long look, like she was trying to see right inside me. But all she said was: 'We'll be all right.'

As the plane descended, the steward came around with a bag for the rubbish. My mother took handfuls of diary and put them in the bag. I put in my juice beaker, threw it, like I was shooting hoops. The oil man stayed asleep, and my mother helped the steward collect his champagne bottles.

The captain made an announcement:

We will be arriving in Heathrow in fifteen minutes.

A few people cheered. I held up my hand to my mother.

'High five, Mom!'

'Right!' She slapped my palm.

Lights started to show in the city below – London, England – and the pressure built in the plane, hurting my ears.

'Do this,' said my mother. She held her nose and shut her eyes tight. It made her look like she was trying not to cry.